EUCALYPTUS

Biblioasis International Translation Series
General Editor: Stephen Henighan

I Wrote Stone: The Selected Poetry of Ryszard Kapuściński (Poland)
   Translated by Diana Kuprel and Marek Kusiba

Good Morning Comrades by Ondjaki (Angola)
   Translated by Stephen Henighan

Kahn & Engelmann by Hans Eichner (Austria-Canada)
   Translated by Jean M. Snook

Dance with Snakes by Horacio Castellanos Moya (El Salvador)
   Translated by Lee Paula Springer

Black Alley by Mauricio Segura (Quebec)
   Translated by Dawn M. Cornelio

The Accident by Mihail Sebastian (Romania)
   Translated by Stephen Henighan

Love Poems by Jaime Sabines (Mexico)
   Translated by Colin Carberry

The End of the Story by Liliana Heker (Argentina)
   Translated by Andrea G. Labinger

The Tuner of Silences by Mia Couto (Mozambique)
   Translated by David Brookshaw

For As Far as the Eye Can See by Robert Melançon (Quebec)
   Translated by Judith Cowan

Eucalyptus by Mauricio Segura (Quebec)
   Translated by Donald Winkler

MAURICIO SEGURA

EUCALYPTUS

TRANSLATED FROM THE FRENCH BY
DONALD WINKLER

BIBLIOASIS
WINDSOR, ONTARIO

Originally published as *Eucalyptus* by Éditions du Boréal, Montreal, 2010.

FIRST EDITION

Library and Archives Canada Cataloguing in Publication

Segura, Mauricio, 1969-
[Eucalyptus. English]
    Eucalyptus / Mauricio Segura ; translated by Donald Winkler.

(Biblioasis international translation series)
Translation of: Eucalyptus.
Issued in print and electronic formats.
ISBN 978-1-927428-37-5 (pbk.).--ISBN 978-1-927428-38-2 (epub)

    I. Winkler, Donald, translator II. Title. III. Title: Eucalyptus.
English IV. Series: Biblioasis international translation series

PS8587.E384E9213 2013   C843'.54   C2013-904438-8

Edited by Stephen Henighan
Copy-edited by Allana Amlin
Typeset by Chris Andrechek
Cover Design by Kate Hargreaves

 Canada Council for the Arts   Conseil des Arts du Canada    ONTARIO ARTS COUNCIL / CONSEIL DES ARTS DE L'ONTARIO

 Canadian Heritage   Patrimoine canadien

Biblioasis acknowledges the ongoing financial support of the Government of Canada through the Canada Council for the Arts, Canadian Heritage, the Canada Book Fund; and the Government of Ontario through the Ontario Arts Council. We acknowledge the financial support of the Government of Canada through the National Translation Program for Book Publishing for our translation activities.

PRINTED AND BOUND IN CANADA

MIX
Paper from
responsible sources
FSC® C107923

*This is for Antoine (seven years old),
my travelling companion in the exploration
of bottomless depths and lost galaxies.*

*He thought that it was loneliness which he was
trying to escape and not himself.*
William Faulkner, *Light in August*

1

On the horizon, pools of water vaporized as he advanced. His hand gripped the wheel, but it was as if it belonged to someone else. For several kilometres, Alberto had been driving oblivious to the fly that was spinning drunkenly, careening off the windows, buzzing furiously. Nor did he notice the bright yellow of the wheat fields rolling by on both sides. He only came to himself when the pickup crossed the old metal bridge over the Bío Bío, where there was a gaggle of children giddy with laughter bobbing along in the river's treacherous current. On the bank, their parents were stuffing themselves with meat off the grill and drinking red wine from plastic cups, while keeping a lazy eye on their offsprings' dangerous games. That's it, he thought, I'm here. He lowered the window to savour the elusive, vaguely clinical odour of the eucalyptus bordering the Pan-American Highway, and told himself that even his knowledge of the southern flora, he owed to his father.

In the rear-view mirror he saw Marco who, his eyes closed, his lips puffy, was resting his forehead on the atlas for children they had found in a Santiago bookstore. Earlier, his son had asked:

"When Abuelo saw me, what did he say?"

"Nothing, he took you in his arms and he rocked you. You were only a baby."

"But Papa, why didn't you take a picture of Abuelo and me?"

"Abuelo doesn't like pictures."

It took a moment before it struck him that he was using the present tense.

"And why doesn't he like pictures?"

"I don't know. That's the way he is."

"Oh Papa, I want a picture of Abuelo and me!"

"That's not possible now. I already told you why."

His son turned his head towards the window, his arms crossed, pouting, and was soon asleep.

Now, making out in the distance the blue and white sign of a gas station, he slowed and stopped in front of a pump. As he turned off the engine, he wondered whether he had made a mistake by borrowing such a gas-guzzler from his uncle. Should he have listened to his mother, who had insisted that he take the afternoon train? Probably. But still reeling from the shock of Anne-Marie's leaving him a few months earlier, he didn't want to be alone with his mother, especially in a train compartment, with the scrutiny of his personal life that was sure to come. And so he had chosen to travel with his son, and to nurse his wounds in peace. What was curious was that from the moment he'd heard about his father, he expected to be overwhelmed. But instead of being overcome with emotion, he'd been mulling over what his Aunt Noemi had said to him over the phone—she who was the only one among his father's brothers and sisters who had stayed on good terms with him. What was this illness that had so rapidly undermined his father's health? Had he himself not spoken to him on the phone barely five months ago, and had not his voice seemed strong and robust?

He shot a glance towards the garage. When he sounded his horn, sparrows hopping about an oily puddle of water flew off in every direction. A man in grey overalls came out, wiping his hands on a rag. He wore his cap so low, almost to his eyebrows, that Alberto could not see his face. When, standing next to the driver's door, he asked what it would be, Alberto said a full tank. The man took the nozzle and, as he bent down to insert it, Alberto saw his profile in the outside mirror. He had the same lined and angular face, the same narrowed eyes, the same indrawn lips, but it was not so much the familiar features as his air of treacherous guile that suddenly brought his father to mind. An unlaced boot propped on a garden chair, a cigarette between the index and middle finger, the vision assailed him for the umpteenth time, larger than life, while behind him between two hills the sun set, crimson and fatalistic. The unflinching eyes, deceptively lazy, with just a glimmer of light at the corners, spoke of an ironic resignation, and an irascibility that could surface from one moment to the next. And so although he knew the scene was imagined, he distinctly heard, in a soft voice that was never his father's, as if he had at last let down his guard: "We never understood each other, Alberto."

The man was holding out his hand. He twice beckoned with his thin, oil-stained fingers. Alberto fumbled in his pockets and brought out two ten-thousand-peso bills. The man turned his back and disappeared into the darkness of the garage. After a moment, seeing that he was not going to come back with any change, Alberto started the engine and made his way back onto the Pan-American.

WHEN THE PICKUP entered the outlying neighbourhoods of Temuco, Alberto took no notice of the election posters glued to the telephone poles, with either the lunar face and tired eyes of Francisco Huenchumilla, the mayoral candidate for the *Concertación*, or the open gaze and parted hair of Miguel Becker, candidate for the Alliance party. All he saw, through the smog here and there perforated by the sun, were the first little wooden houses, greyish yellow, tilted to the side as if about to collapse. These dwellings reminded him of another arrival in Temuco in the company of his father. It was 1990, no more than a month after the return of democracy. For the first time since his exile to Canada in 1974, his father was setting foot in that city so dear to his heart. As for Alberto, he would be in Chile only briefly, as he had decided to remain in Montreal to pursue his studies while his parents and brother returned to the

4

country of their birth. Under Alberto's attentive gaze his father, bright eyed, at the wheel, noted every detail, while the mother and brother were slumped in the back seat. Yes, he thought, Papa preferred this city to many of the people around him. But above all, he thought: Yes, it is now that the family is breaking up, decomposing like molecules being brought to the boil, and we are scattering to the four corners of the American continent.

Now, as he drove along the Avenida Alemania, past its expensive houses with wrought iron fences and vast gardens and the monochrome condominiums rising up behind, it occurred to him that the reunion of the four members of his family, a reunion he had so often longed for over the past years, and even more intensely during the last four months, was no longer possible. As he parked the truck in front of the slope-roofed house of his grandparents, he was overcome by a sense of emptiness. Yes, that is what he felt, because it would not be until a few hours later, when he would see the scar on his father's remains, that he would be overwhelmed by grief. Standing on the sidewalk he scrutinized the house for a long time, with its warped roof, its peeling paint, and dust encrusted window panes, only a shadow of what it once had been. He helped Marco out of the vehicle.

Alberto rang, but no one came to the door. He turned the knob and cautiously entered the living room, where the silence was broken only by the clock that marked off, painfully, the passing of every second. He and Marco went from one room to another and soon discovered, upstairs, a form on a bed under a white embroidered eiderdown. In a corner, in front of the hazy light drifting in through window, a woman wrapped in a *manta* dozed, her profile noble, her skin shrivelled. It was Abuela. When he crept around the bed, Alberto saw the thin and livid face of his father, who seemed to have aged enormously. Someone had dressed him in a white shirt he would never have consented to wear when he was alive. What is more, he was in a position that did not suit him, lying on his back with his hands clasped over his stomach, giving him a meditative air. When, by his side, Marco froze, fearful, Alberto pulled him gently towards him. After a moment, in a touching gesture, his son bent his ear to the corpse's chest, as if to confirm that the heart had well and truly stopped.

"Oh, Abuelo ..." said Marco, raising his head.

Then, dizzyingly, his memory disgorged multiple images of his father. He remembered when he was always neatly dressed, the hem of his white tunic thrown up by his rapid strides. He remembered him in a plaid shirt, construction boots always unlaced, when, exhausted, he pushed open the door of their cramped apartment in the neighbourhood of Côte-des-Neiges. He saw him bearded, his hair long, just as in the photos taken when he was going to university and living only for meetings and demonstrations. Finally, he remembered him from the last time he had paid him a visit, wearing a rippling leather hat with a lasso hanging from his waist, sharp-eyed, taciturn like the peasants around him on the farm he ran with an iron fist. He thought again of all these roles his father had played, and could not connect them.

How he would have liked to collect his thoughts, to lay down at the foot of this body the confused tangle of emotions at work within him!

When Abuela began to moan, doubtless in the throes of a nightmare, Alberto took Marco by the hand and left the room.

ONCE IN THE COURTYARD, Alberto didn't see him right away, because he was off to the side, out of the sun, under a corrugated iron roof. Enrique, his father's youngest brother, an adopted son whose family name, Araya, had stuck to him like a birthmark, had been skin and bones just a few years ago; now he lifted his arms slowly, breathed through his mouth, and would have had trouble tying his own shoelaces. An axe over his head, the other hand holding a log, he looked more and more like his boss, thought Alberto, remembering the fleshy butcher with white hair and a sharp tongue. It seemed to him, from where he stood, that the axe grazed Araya's fingers when it fell. The high grass, colour of straw, had overgrown everything in the courtyard: bald tires, the old body of a Coccinelle with shattered windows, tools, iron bars. What would Abuelo have thought of this neglected yard, he who had succeeded in restoring the house? Too old to go on working the land, his children having

7

left it, he had acquired it to bring the family together again, something he had achieved in part, since four of his daughters came to live here with their husbands and children. That was what made it possible for him to live out the last of his days in something of a domestic circle, as he had hoped.

"You've seen the weather?" asked Araya, raising his eyes.

When Alberto looked at the sky, he had to squint.

"You ever remember heat like this in October?" Araya went on. "I'm telling you, the planet is all topsy-turvy."

With disturbing ease, like a knife cutting through *quesillo*, the axe split the log in two. Araya stood the axe head on the concrete, looked Marco up and down, and balanced another log on the stump.

"No point looking for anybody."

He leaned over and spat to the side.

"Noemi's left for the *campo*," he added, referring to his father's land. "And to Cunco too I guess, for the legal papers… I figure you must be happy to be back. That makes what, four years that you haven't been to see us?"

"Four years. Exactly."

"So tell me. You still freezing your balls off in the land of hockey?"

Alberto smiled, and as Araya launched into a playful description of a fight during a game he'd seen on TV, he thought to himself that the last time he was here his uncle did not have this ragged beard now growing like a weed.

"And the little one's mother?"

As Alberto did not reply right away, Araya said:

"You know, I'm separated too."

When he smiled mockingly, his double chin was more noticeable. So he'd heard about his recent marital problems. But who had talked to him, since even his father had known nothing about it. His mother?

"There's nothing to be ashamed of in that, you know…"

"Did I say I was ashamed?"

"You really look like one, don't you?"

"What?"

"A writer. You know, I can't stand novels. But when I come across a writer on TV, I stay on the channel. Those guys fascinate me, they have something, I don't know what exactly… Seems you have to teach too?"

Alberto nodded yes, thinking: "He's up on everything. He knows I don't like teaching. That it takes up all my time, making me work late at night on my hypothetical novels, once Marco is asleep." To change the subject, he asked him when the burial would be.

"If you ask me, there won't be many people at the cemetery," Alaya replied.

"Why do you say that?"

"He didn't know how to make himself loved, your old man. He didn't have the knack. And what are you going to do with his land? You know it goes back to you, right, to you and your brother?"

"I don't know yet. We'll see."

"But you know what he had, right? They said 'internal hemorrhage.' You believe that?"

Alberto was suddenly all ears, but he kept quiet.

"In my opinion," Araya went on, "he hurt himself and didn't deal with it. And what happened happened. He went down. And so fast, my friend…"

He laughed openly, in a way that clearly gave him satisfaction.

"You know me, I'm not like the others here, all religious fanatics. Still, the way he died makes you think. God's punishment? You can't rule that out."

Alberto tolerated Araya's gaze for a long moment, then he beckoned Marco to come near. Side by side, they walked towards the house.

"Hey, wait… Wait, I said!"

Alberto stopped in the doorway and slowly turned around.

"Come here," Araya continued, "Sit down… Sit down, I tell you!"

Alberto dropped his son's hand and, reluctantly, lowered himself onto the sofa leaning against the house's brick wall.

"I understand you, you know," said Araya. "Me too, when I was younger I idolized your father."

"I don't idolize my father."

"Are you sure? Anyway, there's one thing you can't deny. Roberto ran away from Chile. You understand? He ran away. That's what's behind everything."

10

"He left because his life was in danger."

"He left because he was just waiting to leave. Your father was ambitious, very ambitious. He dreamed of the North."

"I see you didn't know my father."

Araya smiled with a falsely conciliatory air.

"Listen, let me tell you something. Okay?"

At first Alberto wondered if he should just leave, but astonishingly, as the other talked, he found himself more and more rooted to the spot out of curiosity and lassitude. He listened as Araya talked about the political circumstances surrounding his parents' return to Chile at the beginning of the 1990s, when Patricio Aylwin's coming to power inspired a wave of hope. He was going to rebuild the country, to restore dignity to the people who had been held in contempt by the military regime, we were going to open ourselves to the world, and to welcome hundreds and thousands of exiles with open arms. In point of fact, after seventeen years of dictatorship, just telling the population that it was now free was enough to raise its spirits. And then bit by bit the celebrations dissolved into day-to-day life. And with the simple power of words, Araya conjured up Roberto getting down from a train that had arrived from the capital. While a morning mist wrapped the streetlights in an aura of mystery, his father advanced along the sidewalks of Temuco, trailing a small black suitcase on wheels, oblivious to the taxi drivers and their honking.

11

He passed in front of the Pinto *feria* where the empty stalls, under the gallery's deep arcades, stood next to piles of wooden crates, and where the wind swept cardboard boxes along the ground and sent a newspaper flying into the air. He passed through the centre of town, past the university he had attended forty years earlier and that no longer had the same name, and turned onto Calle San Martin leading west.

"He walked like that," said Araya, "from the centre of town to here. As if there were nothing to it, a good hike. In front of the house he must have noticed all the cars double-parked. Then he went up the path. He rang the bell, but there were so many people that nobody heard. He pushed open the door, and that's when I saw him. It was not the first time I'd seen him since he'd been back in the country, and right away I was astonished to see how much the news seemed to have affected him. His eyes were frozen, shining, like those of a madman. People went up to him and embraced him. They pretended to be surprised that Carmen had not come with him, but they knew their marriage was going from bad to worse. I remember, he took a good look at the weeping women. It's true they were laying it on a bit thick, swaying from side to side, and crying as if they were really sad that the old man was gone," Araya said, smiling. "It must have reminded him of his childhood. In a corner, the old man's friends, those mad for Yahweh, dressed in black and all wearing skullcaps, were talking softly. Then he went up to the coffin. I was watching him, and I saw right away that he had something in mind. And just like that, there, in front of everybody, the man opened the coffin's lid. The women stopped weeping, discussions shut down, and they all threw themselves at him. Don't you know, you don't do that, it's forbidden! But he'd had time to open the coffin, and we all saw the old man's bony face and silver hair. That gave me a jolt, because he had a gentle air about him, something you never saw during his lifetime. Then, as Noemi, I think, was taking him by the hand, Roberto fell to the ground, all at once, just like that, knocking his head against the coffin. Four of us picked him up and carried him to the sofa."

Alberto had no trouble imagining his father opening his eyes, laid out on the sofa. He imagined him blinking on seeing the maid bent over him, fanning him, while behind him the weeping women had resumed their plaints. His father got up, unsteady, and went into the kitchen, where sitting beside the wood stove he found Abuela, her eyes motionless, muttering away as usual. He knelt down before her and listened: "Why is the house full of strangers," she complained. "*Mamá, soy yo*," he said to her, but she kept on moving her lips, gazing into space as if she had just lost her sight. He rose and placed a kiss on his mother's brow, before Noemi burst in to announce that it was time to leave for the synagogue.

Outside, the mist deepened his melancholy, as he held up one corner of the coffin and onlookers joined the procession. At intersections, traffic stopped to let them pass. He recognized the synagogue immediately, the two-storey stone building with its balcony and modest dome on which one could make out a Star of David. In a city so eager to tear everything down, this dignified building is a kind of miracle, thought Roberto.

As the ceremony began, he was surprised to find that his Hebrew came back to him quickly, but he soon tired of the rabbi's psalms. He cast his eyes around and studied the faces that once peopled his childhood, today ravaged by time and the South's harsh climate. Aunts, uncles, distant cousins, friends of the old man, his colleagues and his suppliers, in short Temuco's entire Jewish community had turned out. Who would have thought that the old man was so much appreciated? And Araya reported what he had learned from his sister Noemi: that towards the end of the ceremony the rabbi, by a coincidence that left Roberto speechless, had proclaimed aloud what he himself had been trying to express for days: "To turn your back on his past is as vain as wanting to fell a tree with your bare hands."

When Araya paused, Alberto interrupted him:

"Fine. But what are you getting at with all this?"

"Just be patient. The next day, all the brothers and sisters were seated here, in the dining room. At one end, her eyes half open, Mama smiled, she barely understood what was going on. At the other end, Noemi held an envelope in her hands. Everyone understood immediately, you could have heard a fly on the wing. Noemi coughed, she tore open the envelope, and brought out a sheet of squared paper, on which I recognized the old man's elongated, flowing script. She began reading. The letter went something like this, in the old man's inimitable style. (Here he assumed a stentorian voice): 'So as to honour the will of Yahweh, so as to give thanks to my beloved family and to ensure our perpetuity in this lost corner of the world, I leave...' Noemi stopped reading, not believing her eyes, then she pulled herself together and went on in a halting voice: '...I leave all of my assets in the hands of Roberto, my son, who is free to dispose of my inheritance as he deems best...' Can you imagine? I, who in his last years, had spent whole days with the old man, talking to him, going with him to fetch his wine at the *botelleria*, sometimes even reading to him from his Zionist journals, I was dumbstruck, I have to admit. What had I done to him to deserve this slap in the face? What had Roberto done to so enter into his good graces? I decided to find out. And you know what? Nothing. Roberto had not lifted his little finger for the old man."

For a few moments, his shoulders hunched, wholly absorbed in his story, he looked at Alberto without seeing him, his gaze passing through him as if he were a ghost.

"The truth," he continued in an absent voice, "is that in that instant Roberto was as stupefied as we were. He hadn't seen it coming, either."

Roberto got to his feet, walked shakily into the middle of the living room, leaned on the back of an armchair.

He felt, thought Alberto, everyone's eyes burning into his back. Until that day his life had been a woeful mistake, a comedy with no rhyme or reason. The old man, having understood him, wanted to give him a chance to redeem himself. Was that it?

"Don't worry, everyone will get his fair share," said Araya, trying to mimic Roberto's voice. "That's word for word what he said, you can check it with the others. And then everyone went to embrace him."

The following Saturday, stuffed like sardines into two white vans Araya had borrowed from his boss, they all left, the dozen of them, for the old man's land. It had been years since any of them had been back there. Everyone was in a good mood in the vehicle where Araya was riding, and where Roberto found himself as well. Crude jokes flew back and forth, along with some pointed jibes. They sang *tonadas* from the South, vaunting the serenity of country life, the virtues of nature in its lushness, the proverbial hospitality of people from the region. Irony warred with nostalgia as, with humour, they relived childhood's hard times, lingering over their daily ordeal: nearly four kilometres to navigate on foot, through the forest, to get to school.

"But as for Roberto, *nyet*," said Araya. "He didn't say a word."

When the van's tires started spinning in the mud at the bottom of a slope, everyone got down to continue on foot. They scaled hills strewn with stones, stepped over clear streams whose gurgling never stopped, asked permission to cross through corrals where wary sheep gave them a wide berth. Along the way most complained of sore feet, and took long pauses, sitting on rocks or lying on the pastures' green grass. At the top of a mound dividing two properties, Roberto stopped, shading his eyes with his hand. He recognized far off, dominating another height, the old man's white house with its tile roof and the forest of eucalyptus surrounding it.

"Suddenly, I confess, I almost stopped breathing," said Araya. "The house was magnificent. We had been wrong to resent it. It was all because of the old man and his stubbornness."

Once on the property, Araya saw that the structure needed a good coat of paint, that inside a film of dust covered the rustic furniture, that the arable land was overgrown with weeds, and that the eucalyptus trees had attained dizzying heights. But those were only details requiring minor work. Opening the shutters, Araya was taken aback by the extent of the old man's lands, with its meadows for cows and a dense eucalyptus forest. To the left, he could make out in the distance the high wooden steeple of the church at Cunco, the little town where, as children, they went to school; to the right, nearer by, on the edge of a wood, a group of houses and straw huts belonging most likely to a Mapuche community.

In the kitchen people bustled about, while in the garden a simple wine in a carafe was passed around the table. As people were asking what had happened to the Jewish families in the environs, Araya saw Roberto slip away behind the house. Stealthily, he followed him, saw him turn around several times, and plunge into the trees. He wandered about for a while, looking up, as though in contemplation of the odorous eucalyptus greenery overhead. He stopped at the foot of a steep slope to admire the view: a happily babbling river, shimmering, flowed rapidly along past a scattering of rocks and their necklaces of foam.

"What do you suppose he was thinking about?" asked Araya, his eyebrows raised. "Of going fishing with the old man, when we were ten years old? We pulled our jeans up to our knees, we held our bamboo fishing rods in both hands as if our lives depended on it, and we followed the old man's instructions to the letter. After all, he was a master fisherman."

Suddenly, Roberto placed the flat of his hand on the trunk of a tree and lowered his head. Then he fell to his knees, his arms trembling.

"Yes, he was sobbing like a child," said Araya, lost in the memory. "I'd have given anything to know what was going through his mind at that moment. If you ask me, he saw what a huge mistake he'd made, leaving the South thirty years earlier. It came to him that life can be unjust and cruel if you take too long finding your way. He thought about all the time he had lost, and he cracked."

Alberto had a clear vision of his father rising, dazed, his face wet with tears, hesitant in his movements, powerless to stem the flood of emotion that swept through him.

"As he started back," Araya went on, "I understood everything, and the next days proved me right. That's when he made up his mind. That afternoon, as if it were of no particular importance, he informed us of his decision to sell the land. Of course, on the one hand, we were sad. We were going to lose our own little paradise, part of the family history would be gone forever. We were not oblivious to that. But on the other hand, many of us had serious financial problems. Why hide the fact? The South is not what you see on television, this Eldorado where you get rich overnight. I wanted my share, I'm not ashamed to say so."

Alberto easily imagined the twelve brothers and sisters eating in silence, under a gentle sun, while a mild and perfumed breeze stirred their hair. From time to time they clinked glasses, their cheeks flushed from wine, from fatigue, and from nostalgia. Someone brought up Roberto's heroics at football, long ago. Another remembered his fondness for lamb, which had him holding onto the handle of the spit so as to be able to bite into the roasting animal as soon as the old man was out of sight. Finally, there was his constant thirst that woke him at night, forcing him to go out and kneel over the rain barrel. Roberto listened to these reminiscences without turning his head towards any of the speakers.

Three days later, Araya, like the others, received a registered letter from a notary, explaining that since

Roberto was the only lawful owner of the land, it was pointless, legally, to oppose him. The letter, brief, written in a direct, unadorned style, ended by wishing them peaceful and prosperous lives.

"That's your father," said Araya. "That's who he really was."

His cheeks burning with shame, Alberto lowered his eyes.

"Of course, I was furious," said Araya. "You wouldn't have been, in my place? I know you know the rest, your father told you. The truth is that I went to see him several times so we could talk. And you know what he did? He set his dogs on me. Look," he said, rolling one of his sleeves up to the elbow.

On his forearm Alberto saw a vague calligraphy of scars, like a child's scribbling.

"That's why you wanted to burn down the house?" asked Alberto.

Araya raised his eyes.

"What did you expect me to do? Just sit there and keep my mouth shut? I wanted him to pay for what he was able to do because no one dared to face up to him!"

He paused.

"*Hijo de puta*," said Araya. "He'd hired a guard. A brute. A Mapu. He laid into me like I was ..."

Fixed on the wild grass, his eyes shone. He gritted his teeth.

"A man who does that, for me there's something wrong with him. A brother who does that, don't ask me to go to his funeral."

20

2

In the middle of the afternoon, tired of waiting for Noemi to come back, tired of the stale odour in the house, Alberto took off in the pickup with Marco. His elbow propped on the open window, he watched, through the rear-view mirror, the light wind at play in his son's hair. When he turned into the Avenida Pablo Neruda, a flash of sunlight created a blinding spot on the windshield, with a rainbow-coloured aura. He passed square after square, and although on many of them youngsters were playing football or marbles, although the benches shone bottle-green, although no litter was lying about, they all seemed drab, desolate. Was it the concrete covering the ground? Or the smog that, like an ulterior motive, darkened the city in full daylight?

He parked the pickup in front of a glass building, in which were reflected the movie theatre's heavy columns, encrusted with dirt. He bought some fried cheese *empanadas*, Marco's favourite, in a nearby grocery store, and they ate them in the shade of a palm tree, on a bench in the Plaza de Armas. As the fountain shot its jet of water towards the sky in a deafening cloud, he scanned an election poster on a lamppost. "Francisco Huenchumilla, Concertación candidate for mayor of Temuco. *Para un ciudad próspera.*" He wondered if Temuco had ever had a native mayor. Behind them, music from another time, childlike and gay, drifted into the square. A man with a hand organ was drawing all eyes. On his shoulder, a monkey munched peanuts and made faces. When he saw Marco watching the show, wide-eyed, Alberto remembered his first impressions of the city when, after having left Chile at the age of four, he returned with his family. At the time everything seemed dirty and old-fashioned; the cars, the excessive pollution, the shifty faces of the street children, the cadaverous features of the women kneeling on the sidewalk, selling Kleenex or *mote con huesillo*. And then, during the same visit, he went from one extreme to the other: he suddenly felt as if he were being reunited with a buried part of himself. He didn't want to leave. But this honeymoon didn't last: people, his extended family above all, made him understand that he was not quite one of them, that in certain respects, perhaps the most important, he was too *gringo*, a remark they let drop, sometimes in jest, at other times in all seriousness. Since then, he had never felt at home either here or back there.

A little girl, her hair held back with pink ribbons, was walking with her mother, a balloon in her hand. He bought one for Marco, and made a knot for him at his wrist with the string; from that point on his son kept his eyes on the balloon, a smile on his lips. They strolled, and soon came on itinerant sellers of every age, set up in front of a shopping centre, behind wool blankets on which were displayed miniature tanks, lighters, ballpoint pens, underpants. Alberto told himself that Araya's story was not at all surprising. He was like that, his father, totally unpredictable, loving to spring surprises and to make a scene, seeking always to protect his moral and material independence.

"And what are going to do now your papa's dead?" asked Marco.

The question pulled him up short.

"Don't worry about me."

And he tried to smile.

"Fleurette says we go up to heaven when we die."

Fleurette was his schoolteacher.

"You think Abuelo's going to heaven?"

"If he behaved well, yes. If not, perhaps no."

"Did he behave well?"

Alberto shrugged his shoulders.

Then, a bit farther on:

"Papa, but why did he die, Abuelo?"

He met his son's eyes.

"Are you going to die one day, too?"

He nodded, yes.

Seeing his son's concern, he added:

"Don't bother about that. It won't be for many years. We've lots of good times ahead of us."

He gripped his hand a little more tightly.

BACK IN HIS GRANDPARENTS' HOUSE, he went upstairs with Marco to the room where his father was laid out. Abuela, still sitting in front of the window, raised her head and blinked her eyes when they appeared, her wine-red *manta* accentuating her slumped shoulders. She stared at them, knitting her brows, then with a movement of her chin she ordered Alberto to introduce himself. When he revealed his identity, she repeated to herself, "Roberto's son," as if she no longer remembered Roberto but didn't want to admit it. After a moment, as Alberto became conscious of the dim light surrounding him, she asked him curtly to leave, because the real Alberto was a boy living in Canada "who's no bigger than that," she said, stretching out the fingers of one hand. He replied that he was the boy, that he had visited her four years earlier. But she made a dismissive gesture with her index and middle fingers, indicating that he should leave. Then he took out of his pocket a watch with a chain, a present from his grandfather, went up to her and held it out. She took it, weighed it, and stared for a long time at the motionless hands, as if memories were working their way bit by bit up to the surface of her mind.

"It doesn't work anymore?"

"For the last few days, it stops and starts. It has to be repaired."

She gave it back to him, and venturing a smile, she said:

"It's really you, Albertito?"

He held the watch and got on his knees at her feet. With her rough fingers, she patted Alberto's hair and cheeks. He looked at her face, which, despite her yellowed eyes, despite the ravages of time, brought back to him a torrent of memories, of when he was Marco's age and she kept him with her for entire days, before the dictatorship chased them out of the country again.

"You look more and more like Roberto," she said, mussing his hair. "Do you have his character, too?" she asked, teasingly. "*Ay, Dios mío*, I hope not!" she added, smiling.

He returned her smile and pushed his face up against her skirts. He felt her own special odour attack his nostrils, one of wool, of tenderness, and of a madness she would not concede. He kept his eyes closed, persuaded that when he opened them he could remove himself from this oppressive climate of mourning.

She gestured to Marco that he should come near. Caressing his hands vigorously, as if she could not believe the softness of his skin, she asked him where his mother was. When the child explained that she had stayed in Canada, she looked at Alberto the way she used to when she was going to scold him.

"I'm not wrong, then?" she said. "You are like Roberto?"

Continuing to pass her hands through his curly hair, she raised her eyes to the ceiling and, in a stronger voice, as if she were addressing a large audience, embarked on a confused tirade against men and the desires that possess them like evil spirits. An evil she traced back to her dead husband, and her husband's father, and his father before him. She went on with her monologue, digging deeper into the family's past, and recalling, as she never failed to do, their ancestors' arrival from Europe in the second half of the nineteenth century, from an idyllic village called Monastir, today Bitola, at the heart of Macedonia. And Alberto was treated to the entire narrative of the family's founding, only now it was timely, because although he knew it was a romanticized version, he needed to hear this story of emigration, of a flight by boat against the backdrop of a great conflagration, of the persecution of the Jewish community, and the decadence of the Ottoman Empire. Then, losing the thread of what she was saying, as if suddenly she had come back to herself and the weighty concerns of the present, she went silent. Her eyes darted this way and that, while at last tears ran down Alberto's cheeks.

"YOU KNOW THEY KILLED HIM, don't you?"

This was less a question than a blunt assertion.

"What?"

"I said they wanted to hurt him and someone killed him."

Alberto stopped blinking.

"*Abuela*, you can't just say things like that, without proof."

"What do you think? I've got proof, a whole lifetime's proof!"

Alberto sat back on his heels.

"Listen, all the Venturas have iron constitutions. You must know that. Look at your grandfather's brothers and sisters. They all lived to almost a hundred, no? Your father was not a Magallanes. Like Noemi, for example, with her delicate health. He was a Ventura. Even as a child, he never got sick."

Marco, seated near her on the wood floor, was all ears.

"What they're saying makes no sense," she burst out. "There's something wrong there."

"What do you mean?" asked Alberto.

"I mean he didn't get sick, I mean someone is lying. I know it, I feel it…"

She added:

"Wait, wait a little."

And she talked about how she and Roberto always spoke on the telephone every Sunday, just after dinner. Alberto then remembered his father pacing up and down the hall, the receiver held to his ear, holding the base in one hand, the wire trailing on the carpet of their Côte-des-Neiges apartment, while Alberto's mother, lying on the bed, listened in while pretending to leaf through a magazine, jealous, Alberto thought, of the close bond between her husband and her mother-in-law, but never saying a thing. Meanwhile he was living his own life, cloistered in his bedroom, his den, propped against the headboard, with his cassettes, his books, and already his first writings.

"If he'd really been sick, he would have told me. But the last Sunday before he died, he didn't phone. For the very first time, on that day, we didn't talk. I sat by the telephone for hours, and when I saw the sun set, I knew something had happened to him."

Alberto's heart was speeding up, but still he ventured:

"Maybe he wasn't feeling well and didn't want to worry you?"

"Didn't want to worry me," she repeated, disdainfully, shutting her eyes. "Do you know how far back those Sunday telephone calls go?"

And without waiting for an answer, triumphant:

"Forever! They go back to the morning he left the house from one day to the next. He hadn't even started to shave."

Alberto felt a prickling on his face, as if an imaginary hand were having its way with him, sticking him with sewing needles. Meanwhile Marco edged closer to his great-grandmother, the better to hear.

"It was a weekday," she said. "It was raining cats and dogs. Aside from your grandfather, there was only Roberto and me at the farm."

Roberto raised his head to see, over the cow's black back, behind the thick curtain of rain that made the fodder all the more odorous, the old man mounting his horse, surrounded by his men. He pulled at Estrellita's reins, the horse unusually wild that day, in a filthy mood, as the rain pelted down like bullets onto her straw hat. Roberto stared at his father and saw clearly that his lips were moving. What was he doing? Ordering the animal to calm itself? Was he trying, as was his way, to frighten it a little by speaking rapidly? From time to time the old man turned his head towards Roberto so that he would come and help, or so Roberto thought, but he couldn't be sure: his eyes were hidden by his hat's rim.

"Roberto wasn't going to school?" asked Marco.

"He'd repeated his year, and your great-grandfather made him work on the farm. For a whole year. He got up at four in the morning and went to bed at seven at night, dead from fatigue. He went off to pile hay and saw that others were doing their homework or having fun. I said to your great-grandfather: 'All right, he understands, let him go back to school.' But your great grandfather barked: 'Don't interfere. I want him to beg me, next year, to be sent to school.'"

"It's curious, he never talked about that," said Alberto.

"That doesn't surprise me," said Abuela, repressing a smile.

Roberto continued working at the cow's teats. God in heaven, she seemed truly feverish, with drool flowing from her mouth and an eye bizarrely closed, invaded by pus. She was giving hardly any milk; there was only about a cup in the pail, no more. When Roberto raised his head again to glance towards the old man, he saw Estrellita awkwardly waving her hooves in the air, with the grey sky behind like thick smoke. Her iron horseshoes were making arabesques. It was with such fright, with such horror, that he followed the graceful, almost human arching upwards of the animal, that he didn't notice that she was landing each time on a sodden light blue sweater. Nor did he see that the men had spread out, knees bent as if ready to pounce, forming a circle around the old man, the mare, and this worker on the ground who was now hiding his face with his forearm.

After a long minute, perhaps two, Roberto finally realized that behind the shafts of rain, the hooves were sinking themselves into the stomach of the man in the light blue sweater, then with time stopped, rising again in slow motion, the better to trample the entrails of the man, who was no longer moving.

"Your grandfather had just told five of his men that he no longer required their services," said Abuela in a strong voice, as if the men in question were in the room. "They became mad, desperate. They threatened him. And Estrellita, that magnificent animal that guessed at everything, defended him tooth and nail."

Paralyzed, Roberto upended the pail with his foot. The little pool of milk spread over the grass, and was instantly diluted by the rain. But Roberto kept his eyes riveted on the scene where, fifty metres away, beside the chicken coop, his father's life hung by a thread. As the animal reared up again, neighing as though delivering itself of a despairing cry, the old man, still in the saddle, but who had inadvertently dropped the reins, tried to regain control in full flight. Roberto saw him, tenacious, doing everything he could to clutch at something. He saw him in the winds gliding by the heights of Llaima's snowy peak; as if gravity itself had abdicated, he saw him in an impossible position: his head almost touching his feet, his arms stretched out, still struggling as his straw hat spun away. Then, as if a magic spell had been broken and reality had got the upper hand once more, he saw him, like a sack of potatoes, drop to the ground and not bounce back.

Thick and obstinate, the rain pounded the old man's body. Estrellita escaped the men, and describing a half moon, took flight. Alberto could easily imagine the old man's employees with their eyes on the motionless body, glancing furtively around, suddenly exasperated by the never-ending rain pouring down. All at once the old man moved a hand. An arm. Palm on knee, he tried to rise. Blinking his eyes convulsively, he seemed to be looking for his hat. Erect, he pivoted, swayed, oblivious of the men as they tightened the circle around him.

"If I remember well," said Abuela, "we had just become associated with Araucania Madera. A British company. They supplied us with machinery. We supplied the labour. That's when we planted our first eucalyptus."

It's true, they were among the first to associate, thought Alberto, with the company that now called all the shots in the region. Abuela looked at him sternly, and went on, as though in reply to his censorious and disappointed gaze:

"Then, people didn't yet know this tree. Those few who had heard about it only knew that it came from Australia and that it grew with phenomenal speed. And that in the old country, in Europe, they paid generously for the paste made from eucalyptus. And in fact," she continued, a smile crossing her face, "in less than ten years, many fortunes were made thanks to this magical and odorous tree that Yahweh had been kind enough to place in our path. And yes, your grandfather was one of them. And then, what? What did we do that was so bad? The Levys and the Kalderóns, didn't they do as much? You know, when I hear people today complaining about this tree, it makes me laugh. Some, it's true, went too far, and they paid the price: the tree ruined their land. And yes, it excited the avarice of others. But you have to remember what's most important: it pulled us out of poverty. That's enormous! Really, people have short memories."

Once the workers encircled the old man, Roberto could no longer see him. It was as if he had disappeared. Then, to his left, he heard a whistling, like the lisping cry of the *jote*. He saw his mother, in a long creased skirt, hatless, the rain pouring down her cheeks, advancing purposefully, her face grim, her eye flush with the sight of a rifle.

"I'd been following what was going on from the kitchen window. When I saw that these no-goods wanted to finish off your grandfather, it was as if I were no longer myself. Still, today, I don't exactly remember having taken the rifle from the rack where he stored his guns, nor having gone out under the rain. All I remember is that they turned as one man and froze when they saw me with a weapon."

"They thought that Abuelo had trampled the man on purpose, is that it?" asked Alberto.

Abuela nodded, solemnly.

"They never wanted to admit that it was an accident. That if anyone was responsible, it was them. Because they were the ones who attacked your grandfather and excited the animal. It's true, your grandfather was a stubborn man, often hard with his men. But never," she said in a ringing voice, "would he have intentionally ridden over one of them with a horse. That was not his way of dealing with conflicts. What happened was unfortunate. Really. The man never walked again. Your grandfather suffered from that. But the truth, the real truth, is that these men hated us, they were jealous of what we owned. It's easy to hate the boss, you know, especially when he's Jewish."

In the midst of the deluge, once the men had come to the aid of the wounded worker, Roberto staggered towards the old man. He saw, thought Alberto, the old man's face washed by rain, his hair now straight and shiny. When he went to take him in his arms, the icy gaze of the old man stopped him in his tracks. In that instant, Roberto

33

found his bony face beautiful, with its fine features and the prominent veins zigzagging down his cheeks.

"Your grandfather told him to leave," said Abuela. "He never forgave Roberto for having done nothing to help him. That moment was seared into his memory. Right to the end."

"But what could papa have done?"

"That's what I kept saying to your grandfather. But he always had the same answer: it was his son he wanted to save him. Not me, his wife. Besides, Roberto was good with the rifle. Anyway, much better than me."

She closed her eyes, as though to indicate that what she was going to say was painful for her.

"Your father too, he never forgave him for throwing him out. Every time your grandfather tried to patch things up over the phone, your father hung up on him. And God only knows how many times I tried to reconcile them. I tried everything."

"But despite that," said Alberto, "or perhaps because of it all, Abuelo left him all he had."

Abuela smiled, staring into space. Her mouth opened, but nothing came out, as if she had suddenly changed her mind, as if she was tired of reviving old demons.

"After that," she said finally, "Roberto settled in Temuco. He was never angry with me. He knew I would never put up with any bickering."

With this radical shift in tone, with these brusque words, Alberto understood she was telling him that the discussion was over.

3

lberto swallowed his glass of beer, sitting in front
of a dessert plate on which was resting a small
spoon. Marco was bent over a colouring book
whose pages were crumpled and stained. A few steps
away, the round and placid face of Señora Miriam came
and went behind the steam over the sink. She wore a
white apron, from time to time turned her head towards
Alberto, and, in her musical accent, told him that of late
Roberto hardly ever came any more to Temuco, that
in fact the family rarely had news of him. When they
learned he was sick, ten days before he died, God take
his soul and may he rest in peace, it was a real surprise,
Señor.

She was silent for a moment, and then, as if to change
the subject, while filling a pot with water, she spoke of
the day when Roberto, here in this same kitchen, during
Alberto's last visit four years earlier, had asked Señorita
Anne-Marie to prepare *calzones rotos*. Did he remember?
Marco was just a baby, still at the breast.

Of course he remembered.

"Ah, I tell you," she sighed, "people always disappear too fast."

Without being too obvious, Alberto searched her face to see if she were sincere.

"And how is Señora Anne-Marie?"

She asked the question without turning her head his way, while scrubbing the pot with steel wool. "Very well, thank you," he replied, assuming that other questions would follow, but they did not. "And Señora your mother?"

"She's coming tonight, she'll stay with her sister."

When the bright red Nissan parked behind the truck, Alberto raised his eyes to see, over the little television set and behind the window frame, his aunt Noemi coming up the drive in the transient grey-blue twilight. As soon as she came into the kitchen, her face brightened on seeing them. She kissed them on their cheeks, fussing over Marco for a long time. When she sat down, Alberto noted that she looked tired and that her eyes were red and slightly swollen.

Did Señora want something to eat? It was all right, Miriam, she had a snack on the way. A little coffee? Good idea. And you, Señor?

"Fine."

Señora Miriam dried her hands on her apron, and came towards them with two cups. After a moment, she placed her hand on the back of Noemi's chair, and bent her head towards Marco.

"And the two of us are going to go up and read a beautiful story?"

Marco raised his head.

"I don't want to sleep, Papa."

"Don't worry," replied Señora Miriam. "We're not going to sleep, we're just going to rest our legs, that's all."

Alberto agreed. And so Marco sighed, and reluctantly made his way around the table. He gave a kiss to his father and Noemi, and held out his hand to Señora Miriam. Alberto heard them as they climbed the stairs. "It's true? You don't know the story of little Lucho?"

Noemi rubbed her forearm, as if to ward off any chills to come. With the remote, she lowered the volume of the television set. Her big green eyes shifted from the small screen to the crumbs scattered over the table, which she began to form into a little pile. You wouldn't think she was papa's sister, thought Alberto. And as with every time he saw her after a long absence, he thought again of her three fiancés who died suddenly before the marriage ceremony could take place. As you might expect on Latin American soil, the gossips were quick to spread sordid rumours on her account, and to brand her as a woman condemned to solitude, a dire destiny, and the punishment of God. Fortunately, as someone of strong character, his aunt never paid much attention to what went on behind her back. In any case, when he thought of her, he always saw the same sepia photograph of her in profile, smiling at the little Italian coffeepot steaming on the kitchen stove, with her French cut and the bangs that offset her sad and lively gaze, while in the background a bearded Roberto in a striped and wrinkled shirt read the newspaper, eyes half open as if surprised by the flash. That photo dated from when they were university students sharing a tiny apartment. In a way, it was a faithful reflection of their relationship: Noemi, with her boundless devotion to her favourite brother, would campaign by his side when he ran for the presidency of the Young Socialists at the University of Temuco, and then, many years later, she would become his principal advisor when he was elected to Congress under Salvador Allende. And you, Papa, what did you do for her in return? Even with her, were you an egotist?

"You know who that is, don't you?" said Noemi, nodding towards a chubby, bespectacled face on the television screen.

"Huenchumilla. I saw the posters on the Plaza de Armas."

"He's way ahead in the polls. I'll only celebrate once he's elected, though. Because they could easily assassinate him…"

On the small screen, Huenchumilla waved to the crowd as he walked away from the microphone. Around him, his supporters, dark-skinned for the most part, applauded wildly. When they raised his arm he smiled, a bit ill at ease. The report then turned to a Mapuche leader with an angular and solemn face: "Be careful, it's not because the Concertación candidate is native that he's going to win

38

the vote of all the native people. Fine, Huenchumilla has promised to help the Mapuche people to regain their dignity, but he has to go further. To commit himself, for instance, to negotiations that would give them back their ancestral lands. Because the voters are not fools, they're watching the Concertación very closely. While it claims to be the great defender of this country's underprivileged, just a few weeks ago, near Bío Bío, it inaugurated an open-air dump right in the middle of a Mapuche cemetery. The Alliance? Don't even talk about them, a Pinochetist party, people whose hands are still dripping with blood." Demonstrators now filled the small screen, brandishing banners on which you could read: *Autonomia del pueblo mapuche,* and *Respeto y dignidad.* All of a sudden police on motorcycles appeared, people scrambled, there was a confused ballet of fleeing demonstrators in the midst of tear gas and rubber bullets. When a journalist from the capital, thin with pale eyes, called the demonstrators "terrorists," Noemi grabbed the remote and pressed "Mute."

"'Terrorists.' Did you hear that? Have they fallen on their heads, or what?"

Alberto asserted that Santiago was out of touch with realities in the South, but clearly the discussion did not interest his aunt.

"What a day!" she sighed. "And I think I'm catching a cold, to boot."

As though to make the point, she started telling him about her day in a light, almost cheerful voice, punctuating her sentences with nervous smiles as if to let him know that, despite the circumstances, she was strong and would not be beaten down. She'd first gone to the village of Las Violetas, to the country house, but without Roberto it seemed unbearably sad. Wherever she looked, the trees, the stable, the pasture, the river, she saw only desolation. What is more, and that was strange, none of the neighbours were at home. She tried to find a will, a document, something, but she left empty-handed. She went to Cunco, to the police station. There, after having been made to cool her heels, they finally let her read the report, but not to make a copy, which also seemed strange. The report, two pages that mainly contained information such as Roberto's age and civil status, concluded that there had been "death preceded by a trauma." In short, he hurt himself at the farm and did not go to the hospital, as he had been urged to do. The body was discovered by a certain Raúl, one of his old friends, and he seemed to have died of an internal hemorrhage.

"What?" said Alberto. "How did he hurt himself?"

"The report said nothing about a wound. And the lieutenant just repeated what he'd written in the report. According to him, if Roberto had seen a doctor, he'd still be alive."

Alberto was dumbfounded.

"I couldn't believe my ears," Noemi went on. "But I also said to myself: that rings true, what he says. Remember, Roberto hated going to the doctor."

And in fact, Alberto had absolutely no memory of his father setting foot in a clinic or in a hospital. On the contrary, thinking he knew enough medicine, he treated himself, like the time he hurt his leg while camping, and Alberto, astonished, surprised him in the woods giving himself stitches, hiding so his wife, a trained nurse, would not see.

"Really," said Noemi, "I don't know what's going on."

Señora Miriam was standing in the kitchen doorway, her purse over her shoulder. "The child is sleeping, I'm finished for today, Madame."

"Thank you, Miriam. See you tomorrow."

"Tomorrow, and a good wake, señor, señora." She crossed herself before disappearing from sight in the dark corridor. When Alberto asked her who she was expecting that evening, Noemi replied that she had invited all her brothers and sisters, but she didn't know who would come.

"Listen, did anyone have a grudge against him recently? You know how he was, he broke with everyone for no reason at all."

Without batting an eye, she gave it some thought.

"I don't know, because he never told me anything any more. I don't think he trusted me like before. He came to pick up his mail, we talked about this and that, but we didn't talk really. It was as if, for some mysterious reason, he'd decided to put up a barrier between us. Sometimes we had elevenses together, but I left him alone, I pretended everything was normal. You've been talking to Abuela, right?"

Alberto didn't react.

"Be careful," she went on. "You have to take everything she says with a grain of salt."

"I know, but all the same. He didn't phone her. And that was the first time in half a century."

Noemi swept her eyes over the garish yellow walls.

"This last year, he completely changed. He became very suspicious. Even with me. Many times I tried to make him listen to reason. But it was as if he no longer needed me, as if he wanted to drop me…"

"Don't say that. You know it's not true."

"In fact, when I think, he began to drift away when he met her."

"Met who?"

"Amalia."

"Amalia?"

Their eyes met, and for a long moment, they were silent.

"He never talked to you about her? Damn," she said softly, as if just to herself. "I was sure you knew, because your mother did."

Alberto didn't move a muscle.

She lowered her eyes, while rubbing her hands together.

"He met her at a fiesta. A fiesta in a Mapuche village, very near the house."

While Roberto and the men, bent over, were gathering eucalyptus branches, a boy dressed in a striped wool vest came running towards them, raising a cloud of dust. He asked one of the workers which one was the boss, then he came to a stop in front of Roberto, his mouth half open as he caught his breath. He had almond eyes, a flat nose, and was already thickset, despite his age. He looked down, stammering, and in that Spanish that sounds as if every sentence is a question, he told him that the chief was inviting them to a fiesta that very night. He recited it all in one breath, as if he had been repeating the words all along the way, and before Roberto had a chance to ask him what exactly was being celebrated, the boy vanished behind a long row of eucalyptus.

That night, Roberto had only one idea in his head, to rest his feet on a chair and watch the sun as it set, while sipping a beer. But how would the Indians react if he did not turn up at the fiesta? Reluctantly, he shaved, showered; he would put in an appearance.

In the yard of a single-storey yellow house, men of all ages were drinking around a picnic table. Near the door leading to the kitchen, where several barrels were turned upside down, women were gossiping. Not far off, children were playing football. At the other end of the yard, some old men, seated on a rock or leaning against a post, looked at him with their tired eyes, while a few mentally handicapped individuals wandered about, their eyes to the ground.

A small man, frail, with an olive complexion, came towards him. He introduced himself; he was the chief.

There was something feline about his eyes, his gestures were slow and calculated. The first thing he did was to share with Robert a Mapadungun proverb foretelling thunderclouds for anyone threatening a son of Ngenechen. A warning? A witticism? He held out a glass so they could drink together. The cider was hot and bitter: had it turned to vinegar? Robert took small swallows, wanting only one thing: to leave.

"No, I've never met him," said Noemi. "It seems he's a sly fox. In any case, he knows how to command respect. In his village, the people do everything he wants, without complaining."

Soon, the men's faces took on a haggard, vaguely demented air. In the midst of this assembly, more and more fantastical as the night drew on, the chief stood apart: he drank moderately, his eyes sharp, despite his sickly demeanour. Roberto spent most of the evening talking to him. The chief listened, his head tilted to the side, his hands resting on one knee. When Roberto declared that he was born and had grown up in the area, the chief told him he was aware of it, and that he knew perfectly well who he was.

"And what are you going to do with your land?" asked the chief.

Roberto explained that three-quarters of the land was reserved for the growing of eucalyptus, wood that he sold to the Araucania Madera Company. Business was good, so why change anything? The rest of his land fed forty or so cows that gave milk. "To be honest," said Roberto, leaning into his companion with a smile on his lips, "that's what gives me the most pleasure. I've always wanted to have a dairy farm. Eventually, I'd like to produce cheese."

Perfectly still, the chief studied him with his piercing eyes, as if waiting for him to add something, as if Roberto's words had left him unsatisfied or indifferent, then finally he spat on the ground before whistling in the direction of a burly man who instantly brought them two more plastic glasses filled with cider. Roberto thought to himself that he had perhaps judged these people too quickly. Like everybody else, they amused themselves on weekends, that's all.

Later, as the cider was making his limbs feel heavy and slow, some women launched into a *datún*, a ritual that seeks to cure chronic illnesses. He had witnessed it once as an adolescent along with the old man. The women danced around the *machi*, the healer, who was stroking the hair of an old man in poor health, lying on the grass. When the *machi* began to tap on a *kultrún*, the women brought branches of *canelo* together over the heads of the invalid and the healer. It was then that Roberto spotted a young woman, not unlike the others (she was small, plump, and her black hair fell gracefully to her lower back), but who executed the dance steps with a mirthful air, the flames of the campfire licking at her round face.

"Her age?" Noemi said. "I don't know. Twenty-four, twenty-five."

As Roberto was opening the door of the pickup, he felt someone pulling at his sleeve. The chief told him that he could not leave without meeting his daughter Amalia. When she emerged out of the shadows, Roberto smiled: it was the young woman he'd observed earlier. When she held out her hand, he told himself that he must be confusing desire with reality, because he could have sworn that she was devouring him with her eyes.

"Amalia," repeated Alberto. "And you say she'd been living with him for a year? I can't imagine him with a woman that age. It's as if you were talking about someone else."

"That's how I felt at first," replied Noemi. "I said to myself: what is she looking for, that one? What does she want? But when I saw them together for the first time, I changed my mind. She teased him, taunted him: 'You have a yen for me, eh, *viejito*?' And he looked at her like a child caught in the act. She took his face in both hands and kissed him tenderly on the mouth. You'd think she pitied him. And you know, in a way, that reassured me ... Roberto always needed a woman's company. First, it was me. After, it was your mother. And then it was this girl's turn."

Back home, Roberto lay down on his bed and watched the walls spinning around him. He might very well never see any of those people again. He could forget about the puffed up faces, the desperate smiles. But the truth was, he had enjoyed himself.

The next week, Roberto moved the silo, and sowed oats ("The new manna apparently," said Noemí) on three hectares, just as an experiment. He bought twenty cows and more up-to-date dairy equipment, and adopted a bright stray dog that he baptized Diego.

One very hot day, as he was transporting a load of milk, he turned off the pickup's engine when he saw appear out of nowhere, in the middle of the dry reddish road, the chief escorted by two sturdy men. The window open, Roberto rested his elbow on the doorframe. The old Mapuche stopped level with the front tire, on the driver's side. His eyes on the triangle carved out of the horizon by two hills, a shimmering panorama in the heat, the chief talked of one thing and another, without conviction, almost flippantly. After a while he remarked, as if commenting the weather:

"You made a good impression on my daughter."

Roberto felt a drop of sweat run down his torso. At first he wondered why the chief was talking to him yet again about his daughter. Was he mistaking his own desire for something real, and was this man truly offering him his daughter? When the chief said, softly, as if pronouncing holy words, that in these times when it's so hard to find work, life is difficult, very difficult, especially for young people who can't pay for their education, it seemed as if he were saying that the young girl was looking for employment. Roberto stared at the charred insects on the windshield, pushed up the back of his leather hat, and murmured:

"I'll see what I can do."

The chief gave the door a tap, turned his back, and walked away from the road.

Ten days later, on a morning when the rain was easing up, he again ran into the chief, but alone (what was he doing there?) at about the same spot. This time Roberto was on foot, along with four of his men. The old Mapuche's face was wet with rain, his smooth, greying hair stuck to his temples. He looked ten years younger. Roberto told him, on impulse, that his daughter, if she was still interested, could clean for him twice a week. The chief's only response was an impenetrable smile.

From Amalia's first day Roberto was taken with her bold gait, her vigorous application of the cleaning cloth, her constant humming. The house began to smell good, its former disorder gone. At noon one day, without anyone asking, she prepared a *cazuela* from what was left of an *asado*, and the men greedily gobbled it up. One of the workers exclaimed, a teasing smile on his lips:

"No doubt about it, when a woman runs the house, it's not the same!"

He burped happily; the others followed suit, their eyes puffy from the punishing heat and a red wine that had their heads spinning.

Each week, on the steps of the house, Roberto brought out a roll of bills to pay the employees standing in line. He didn't know quite why, but it pleased him to see them eyeing the thick wad of bills, whether with greed, feigned indifference, or resignation. It was as if tacitly, he was asking them if they were worthy of the confidence he had invested in them.

"The last time I was here," said Alberto, "I saw how he was treating his employees. I was appalled. It seemed as if he was behaving that way just to tell me, 'Here's what I think of your idealism. You knew that, didn't you?' He always regarded me as someone who didn't understand that life is a struggle, a constant competition. I had the feeling that he was harking back, without saying so, to our former differences."

During his brief exchanges with Amalia, Noemi went on, Roberto tried desperately to find subjects of conversation. Do you need soap? Detergent? No, she had all she needed, thank you. Any questions on what you have to do? No, everything's clear, and she turned her back. Even as one of his workers was waiting to be paid, he followed her with his eyes as she moved about briskly between two rows of bushes dotted with small blue fruit, her bound hair, with each quick step, oscillating like a pendulum.

One morning, in the half-light of the stable smelling of hay, Roberto and his men were huddled around a cow collapsed in a corner. The animal, whose eyes were veering rapidly between exhaustion and panic, mooed less and less, as if she sensed that her little one would not see the light of day, or that she herself would not survive. Amalia's head appeared at the doorway in silhouette. She entered and propped the broom handle against the wall, but remained there, hesitant, her body streaked with light and shadow from the sun's angling through gaps in the boards. She moved towards them, knelt, and probed the animal's belly with such precision that everyone turned to her. She positioned herself behind the animal, and inserted her arm, up to the biceps, into the uterus. She ordered the men to help push the animal onto its side, then spent a good half hour trying to unwind the umbilical cord from the calf's foot, sometimes changing the position of the mother, sometimes that of the little one. Once the rear hooves of the calf came into sight, she stood up. The men pulled, grunting. When the calf fell out onto the straw, the sweat-covered men just stared at it, half astonished, half incredulous.

"We were in the kitchen, Roberto, Amalia, and me," continued Noemi. "And Roberto said that when the calf was born, he knew he would do anything for her. At these words, Amalia rose, leaned towards him, and gave him a long kiss."

Alberto could easily imagine the scene, but he thought to himself that his father was playing the role of an older man besotted with a young, impetuous woman.

In front of the stable, Roberto approached Amalia, took her hands in his, and thanked her warmly. He proposed to all that they celebrate the event with a good bottle of red wine. Under a shifting sky, buffeted by a brisk wind, he was agreeably surprised to learn that she had studied agronomy at the same university he had attended decades earlier. After an hour, instead of following his workers into the field, he stayed behind to talk to her about the techniques for inseminating cows. This exchange, rife with technical terms, convinced him, strangely, that they were drawing closer together, that they were part of the same brotherhood.

"He felt like he'd known her forever," said Noemi.

When Amalia left that day, he watched her silhouette disappearing into the distance, and felt his heart pounding. He smiled, because she took him, in all probability, for a likable grampa, while he was building castles in the air. From that point on the green in the corrals was brighter, the blue at the end of the day more incandescent, the murmuring of the stream more musical. He hardly knew her, but he was convinced that she was an exceptional person.

Without being aware of it, Roberto began to treat his employees with more respect. One morning, when the national football team was playing a game, he put the television set outside on a picnic table.

"Thank you, Amalia!" exclaimed one of the workers, a smile on his lips.

She didn't react, but from the kitchen window where she was drying the dishes, she glared back at the worker.

Two days later, Roberto sent one of his employees to the village to fetch a newspaper. On the doorstep, as the day inched towards its end, he scanned the film schedule.

Then, while driving the tractor in the midst of deafening noise, he rehearsed several times over, in a low voice, the question he would pose to Amalia.

Night come, as she was making her way towards the path leading away from the house, he whistled in her direction, as one would call a dog. She stopped, and, her brow furrowed, stood watching him for some time. Finally, when she approached, he proposed to drive her home. She accepted, an ambiguous smile playing across her round face. They didn't talk during the ride. In front of the chief's house, he cut the engine.

"It's ages since I've gone to the cinema. How would you like to see a film with me tomorrow?"

She looked at him sideways.

"I can't."

He was sure he had made a monumental error in judgment. She found him ridiculous!

"The day after tomorrow, I can."

He looked her in the eyes, as if to be sure that she was not mocking him. Her face was solemn and serene.

"Excellent."

That day, in the half-light of a theatre reeking of cigarette smoke, he was treated to one explosion after another and an endless series of car chases, and he spent two hours glancing at his watch. Later, as they were strolling on the Plaza de Armas, she put her hand to her forehead.

"That gave me a headache!"

They looked at each other, sharing the moment. When, a few metres farther on, he confessed that his ears were ringing, and that he felt as if he was getting off a fairground ride, they broke into hysterical laughter.

"In that moment, he thought: Well, maybe I have a chance after all," recounted Noemi. "That's what he said, there, in their kitchen, the day I saw them together for the first time. Amalia just gave him a steady look. And I swear, it was as if she was dying to make a confession."

"What do you mean?"

"I don't know. She's not a bad person, but I don't completely trust her."

Roberto saw, after a moment, that people were staring at them as if they were shocked or disapproving. Then she took him by the hand. Roberto, unbelieving, looked at her: her profile was all dignity.

That night, just a few steps from the chief's house, in the chill, cramped darkness of the pickup, they exchanged their first kiss. Three days later, when Roberto's employees had gone, they threw themselves on the bed in his bedroom, and after swiftly undressing, they made love. All through the lovemaking, Amalia's eyes never left those of Roberto, as if to ensure that he never forget that it was her he was penetrating, as if to tell him that this act would ineluctably lead to others. After a month, not without a certain embarrassment at the beginning, they showed themselves to be lovers in front of the employees, who either avoided meeting their eyes, or hid their discomfort behind awkward smiles. They met Amalia's family, to be sure from the outset that despite their difference in age, they would be offending no one. Then, one chilly morning, she moved in with him, bringing with her only a brown imitation leather suitcase.

"But why, exactly, didn't you trust her?"

"I know, it was just a feeling."

She stared at the mounds of crumbs on the table.

"Sometimes she was very affectionate with him. At others, she looked at him as if she felt sorry for him."

Over the following weeks, Noemi went on, Roberto spent a lot of time in the chief's backyard discussing the community's demands. The chief was cautious, even a bit calculating. But Roberto soon saw that this man was deeply concerned about the future of his people. This devotion, in which the chief sometimes seemed entirely to lose himself, strongly impressed him, and he tried to help him with his initiatives. For hours he held forth on what he knew about different levels of government, realizing at the same time that the country he had known twenty years earlier had changed. And so from meeting to meeting they went over details that each of them explored independently. Very soon, he began to feel that he was part of a large family, of a community that treated him as an equal, that needed him, and that, astonishingly, showed him facets of himself that had lain buried for a long time.

"But …" said Noemi, "she never wanted to give him a child. Because in the end she didn't love him? Because she found him too old? Or perhaps because she reproached him for not being a Mapuche? Maybe she just didn't want a child? Although that's very rare for a young Mapuche."

"And he, did he really want a child?"

"I saw him begging her to give him this child. I saw him go after her, because she ran off when he brought up the subject. That wasn't like him, all that."

Once more, Albert found it hard to believe his ears. Had his father changed that much?

"In time," continued Noemi, "people in the village got used to him. Or at least they pretended to get used to him. They began to greet him, to talk to him. Did he believe that having a child with Amalia would silence people talking about the difference in their ages? In the South, as soon as you stray from the norm, people begin looking at you strangely. And believe me, trying to change people is a waste of time."

For a moment Alberto imagined his father walking side by side with a young Mapuche woman, through a street full of housewives, their string bags filled with groceries, turning away as they passed.

"I have to find this girl," said Alberto.

"Fine, but you should know that around the country house no one knows where she is. The girl has disappeared."

Alberto looked at her, an uneasy gleam in his eyes.

4

Alberto quietly pushed open the bedroom door, and saw his son lying crossways on the bed, the sheets twisted about, half-covering his legs. He took him in his arms, and settled his warm head, full of dreams, on the pillow, before pulling up the bedclothes. He sat at the foot of the bed for a long time, observing his small half-open mouth, his long black eyelashes, and the slow, regular rhythm of his chest rising and falling. His eyes then wandered to the desk against the wall on which a book still sat, and suddenly he felt as though, from one moment to the next, his grandfather was going to sweep into the room and sit down and read, hunched over as was his custom, his eye glued to a magnifying glass. He pricked up his ears and seemed to hear the guttural murmurs issuing from between his thin chapped lips. The room, whose furnishings were more Spartan than in the other rooms in the house (a bed, a desk, and in one corner a checkered canvas suitcase), and whose walls were bare, was an expression, still, of his grandfather's asceticism.

Alberto lay down beside his son, and his stomach against his back, took him in his arms. That made him feel better, much better, but certain as he was that he would be unable to sleep, he didn't notice that his eyes were becoming heavy and that he was slowly slipping into a dark and unstable world. As often happened, in his first dream, he fell into a deep hole, like Alice and the rabbit with the watch. Soon, after a transition that escaped him, he saw himself walking in a deserted street, between old low buildings that formed a narrow corridor. He advanced in the grey half-light, but did not hear his footsteps. From time to time he met passersby he didn't know, who behaved like sleepwalkers. After a while he had the strange feeling that he kept passing the same buildings. He stopped in front of a wrought iron fence, which hid an interior courtyard where two silhouettes came together and pushed apart. He heard long sighs, murmurs, moans. The man's movements were abrupt and cruelly familiar. When a ray of moonlight revealed his profile for an instant, Alberto shut his eyes too late: he'd seen his father's face. He wanted to turn his head away, but he stayed glued to the spot, mesmerized. With avid eyes he watched his father's hand moving slowly upwards along the woman's black panty hose, and heard her increasingly rapid breathing. Then, seeing her moist lips and her face distorted by desire, he recognized his mother as she passed from sexual ecstasy to stifled sobs.

When he opened his eyes, Noemi was leaning over him, shaking him by the shoulder. She asked him to get up, and while in his mind he still saw his mother's face, he heard the *tonadas* being played downstairs. Once more, he glanced towards the still sleeping Marco, and rose to follow Noemi.

SEATED ON THE SOFA leaning against the wall in the backyard, Alberto watched the shadows passing over the high cedars. How many glasses of wine had he drunk? In the midst of the enveloping darkness, pierced here and there by searing shafts of light, he felt as if the guests were moving in slow motion, like goldfish in a bowl. At one end, behind the ghostly smoke from the grill, Araya was turning over pieces of meat, and his shadow, when he bent down, assumed gigantic proportions. From time to time Alberto embraced the family members he knew. Of the twelve brothers and sisters, only three had come: Noemi, Araya, and Hannah.

He told himself that he had to play the game, a bit like his father, who did not dislike these parties. He took care of the grill, was affable, and drank in moderation. Yes, most of the time he behaved like a gentleman, gallant with the ladies, and a joker with the men. He pretended to be impervious to the sidelong glances, envious or disapproving, of some of his brothers and sisters, and the offended silence behind which Abuelo walled himself off. But always, at some unexpected moment, after an inappropriate remark or an ambiguous gesture on the part of one family member, his eyes began to shine with an opaque, pitiless light, his viper's tongue came alive, and all froze. Some became fearful and moved off, others stared at him with increasing animosity. But he, sovereign in his anger, confident that his fit of rage was just, went straight to the weak point of each one. Even physically you changed, Papa, thought Alberto. You became possessed.

He didn't know how it began (perhaps to avoid reminiscing about his father?), but a political discussion was taking place. The years of dictatorship, the Concertación, President Lagos, whom all praised for his diplomatic and conciliatory gifts. But then Araya cut in, clearly not part of the consensus, to say that like all the Concertación politicians, Lagos was a hypocrite. The socialists good managers? Really! Why not let the Alliance run the country? At least their leaders know something about business. Try to make people think you can be both a socialist and a capitalist? What a laugh! What a lie! In the end, Concertación governs the country badly and redistributes the wealth just as badly. So we were better off during the dictatorship? put in Noemi. You're saying we were happier then? Open your eyes, for God's sake! Look at what Pinochet's lackeys did to the country! They sold it out to the Spaniards, the Germans, the English, the Americans ... But seeing Araya's indifference, Alberto assumed that this was a scene the brother and sister had enacted often.

The arrival of Nelly, his father's elder sister, and her husband Gabriel, shifted the focus of the discussion. Alberto got up to greet them. Everything about Nelly, a swarthy little woman with her hair knotted behind her head, spoke of restraint and repression. Her face, deeply wrinkled, was stamped with unhappiness. Forty years earlier she had lost her daughter in a car accident, and she had never got over it. Her husband, whom Alberto always saw with a skullcap, was a big oafish redhead with sparkly green eyes, and a smile permanently affixed to his face. Like his wife he was deeply pious, but by turning to Yahweh he had been able to reconcile himself with the ordeal that had been visited upon them.

After having refused the glass of wine that Noemi offered him, Gabriel sat down beside Alberto. He reached his arm along the back of the sofa, and crossed his legs to put himself at ease. He questioned him about his mother, his brother, his son. He held forth on a number of subjects relating to reports he had seen on television. He asked him, lowering his voice and speaking confidentially, how he was taking his father's death. Alberto replied, still feeling as though he were in a strange dream, that he was surprised to be so affected by the death of this man who had spent his life avoiding his mother, his brother and himself. And the more he found out, the more he realized that he knew him hardly at all. But can one ever know anyone, however close he may be? Gabriel leaned towards Alberto, passed a hand behind his neck, and stroked his curly hair. Suddenly uneasy, his face up against Alberto's, he said they had to talk. And with a jerk of his head, he urged him to follow.

They passed in front of a loudspeaker, then left behind them the noisy darkness of the backyard to find guests in the kitchen, glasses of wine in hand, who moved aside to let them pass.

Upstairs, Alberto saw dim light leaking from under his grandmother's door. They went into the room lit only by a seven-branched candelabra on a chest of drawers. Their shadows on the wall over the bed made it look as if they were watching a film of their own lives. His father's tunic had a golden cast. In front of the window, Abuela, deeply bent over, slept, clutching a pillow against her breast like a little girl with her teddy bear.

He began to see why Gabriel was asking him to place himself at his side, close to the bed. He obeyed. Gabriel took his hand, raised their arms, and while gazing down on Roberto's motionless face: *Night comes on, it's time to sleep my child, come, you are tired, stretch out at last in the comforting arms of nature and eternal rest, sleep well, day is behind you, the stars twinkle in the firmament…*

Over Gabriel's voice, Alberto distinctly heard the coming and going of his own breath. It seemed to him that every expiration lost itself prematurely in the inhalation that followed. Gabriel then gave him a ribbon. Albert followed his lead: slowly he tore it, fully cognizant of the ritual's pointlessness, of the pointlessness of any ritual.

"Now look," whispered Gabriel.

And he stretched out his hand and pulled back the tail of the tunic, revealing his father's legs and his limp sex, shrivelled as a dry fruit. Gabriel, as clinical as a doctor, turned his father on his side, and with a dramatic gesture, his hand spread wide and his fingers extended, displayed a deep scar, like a snake, zigzagging from waist to chest. At first Alberto didn't comprehend what was being shown to him, nor Gabriel's emphatic gestures. His face contorted at the horror of it all, he leaned down to examine more closely the enormous stitches that reminded him of a zipper. He could barely breathe.

When he finally pulled himself together (after how many seconds, how many minutes?), as Gabriel was watching to see how would react, it came to him that the scar was too crude for it to be the work of a surgeon.

"No one knows," said Gabriel. "Only Nelly. We saw it when we were getting ready to dress him in the tunic."

Alberto felt as if the floor was going to open at his feet and swallow him up.

5

lberto sat in the cramped and rubbery cold of the pickup. A line of vehicles stretched out before him in the darkness. His anger of a few minutes earlier had left him, and he was paralyzed by indecision. He had found himself in the humid half-light of the entranceway, facing a massive door with a spy hole in its centre, Marco over his shoulder still in his pyjamas, and his way being blocked. With pleading eyes, Noemi kept repeating that the funeral was taking place the next morning, at the cemetery. She asked him to be careful on the road, and urged him to go to bed as soon as he got back. They would both get to the bottom of this story, all right? Gabriel took him by the shoulders, a limp, coppery lock of hair falling over his forehead: he hadn't shown him the scar to drive him crazy, *niño*, he'd shown it to him so he would find out what happened. Who better than he could shed light on this story? Winking at him, Gabriel hugged him, slapping him hard on the back, and Alberto felt his rough beard against his cheeks.

Seeing that a woman he couldn't identify was watching him from the kitchen window, he started the engine. At first, he drove slowly. At each intersection, automatically, he glanced back through the rear-view mirror at Marco's sleeping face. Once on the highway he sped up so as to be alone on the road, but the streets and parks, lit by the raw light of the car headlights, looked like nothing so much as a dreary theatre set peopled by thugs with bony faces, and itinerant sellers making their way home on foot.

He crossed a bridge that, in the darkness, resembled a steel beast frozen in place for eternity, its frail limbs gangrened with rust. Far off, on the horizon, the opaque shapes of boats swayed this way and that, limned here and there by a sprinkling of lights. They drove by sawmills with their high brick walls, and warehouses where cranes stood motionless. When he saw the little wood dwellings of Padre Las Casas perched on the hill, one leaning against the other, he had the distinct feeling that it would take very little (a sudden wind, a slight shifting of the ground) for them all to tumble into the roadway like so many houses of cards. Then there surged into view the red serpent, undulating, snaking down his father's violated body. The reptile was headless, a long scarlet cylinder twisting at will, lascivious, encrusted on his father's skin. The beast was there, before his eyes. He saw it on the derelict, ill-lit fountain in a square, he saw it when a motorcycle swerved and the headlight dazzled him with its immaculate white glare. And so when he thought he heard a covert exhalation, he almost lost control of the vehicle. A truck coming towards him honked furiously.

Turning away from the driver's volley of curses, he became aware of a silhouette in the passenger seat, sitting with legs spread, a thin grey coil of smoke rising from the cigarette between its fingers. He saw it, in profile, chortling.

"You want to get us killed or what?"

Alberto kept his eyes glued to the road. He heard the laugh again, a hearty one this time. His father's shade took a puff from his cigarette.

"Take it easy Alberto," he said, softly, "No point getting yourself in a state."

Alberto thought: How am I supposed to take it easy?

"There's no point, I'm telling you. It's the most banal story you could imagine. Of no interest, if you ask me."

Alberto exhaled noisily.

"What are you trying to say?"

"I'm saying that I, who thought I was pretty clever, got caught like a chump. Like a clueless greenhorn."

And he stopped laughing.

"Who did that to you?"

"Oh, you'll find out."

Silence again. Then, after a moment, not knowing quite why, Alberto felt his eyes well up.

"Shit. What now?"

Alberto didn't look at him.

"Please, that's not how I raised you ..."

He had to stifle his sniggering.

Alberto realized that he had driven around the square twice, a few streets away from his Aunt Emma. Afraid that his father might vanish, Alberto didn't look at him, and it seemed that he had never seen so clearly what he was, all feigned composure; this game, this façade suddenly seemed so real. He parked his car in front of his aunt's house, circled the vehicle to take Marco in his arms, and shut the door with his elbow. He made his way towards the bungalow, built like its neighbours on a small rise, and saw his mother on the doorstep, looking worried, rolling her eyes. Carmen climbed the steps, and without asking him any questions, opened the door for him.

"WHAT?" SHE CRIED.

Her back propped against the head of the bed, his mother lay before him, her face round, thick, and devoid of makeup. The beige lampshade was a few centimetres above her head. Her wrinkles, at the temples and around the mouth, were like spider legs. She wore what she always wore when he imagined her: a synthetic pink nightgown. She was reclined as if at her ease, but her large brown pupils betrayed her: there was fear in her eyes. Her right arm was out of sight under the covers, but her hand, as if by magic, reappeared beneath Marco's shoulder, as he slept, turned towards the unlit bed lamp.

Alberto repeated what he had just said about his father's scar. Whispering, she asked him who had done that, why and how, but without really giving him a chance to answer. She whispered, he thought, less not to wake Marco, than to be sure that Pedro and Emma would not hear. Pedro could never stand Roberto being talked about in his house. Now silent, she was unmoving, her lips set, dignified, her gaze questioning.

He had come to tell her what he knew, but soon realized, a bit shamefully, that he did not know much. For a long time his eyes roamed over the purple flagstones.

"Perhaps you have things to tell me," he offered. "Did you know about his relationship with this woman? Why didn't you say anything?"

Suddenly his mother's face changed completely.

"What, it was for me to tell you about this relationship? Why didn't he do it?"

She paused, as if really awaiting an answer.

"He didn't say anything because he was ashamed of what he was doing. Because he knew he was behaving badly."

She surveyed the room, triumphant and at the same time wounded. But bit by bit, as if she saw that this self regard was inappropriate, she lowered her eyes.

"I didn't tell you because I didn't want you to judge your father. I didn't want you to learn about how he had taken up with those people ..."

"With the Mapuches, you mean?"

She closed her eyes, then she cleared her throat, as if to stifle some ill-defined feeling that was creeping up on her. In the past, he remembered, he sometimes surprised her lying on the bed in the master bedroom, crying hot tears. He made a point of passing by the room, looking away.

But over the last ten years, she had hardened: tears almost never came. She began by talking about a night when she was sleeping alone in her Santiago apartment, a few months after her final separation from Roberto. A night when the phone rang, echoing through the rooms, half-empty because Roberto had kept for himself most of the furniture. A long conversation ensued, disjointed, full of incomplete sentences and hesitations, and punctuated by nervous exhalations on the part of his father. He was then living alone in the South, in the country house, persuaded that his view of the world was incompatible with that of others, especially his wife. It seemed he was seeking, not so much advice as the sympathetic ear of his "best friend," as he called her when he left her, looking for a way to spare her, but in fact only wounding her even more. As the telephone conversation proceeded, she began to take in what he was trying to say:

"Your father had found himself at the far end of his land that day. You know, high up, where the grass hardly grows. He was driving the pickup, full speed. From time to time, clouds of smoke obscured the windshield. Behind him the blue of the sky made his eyes smart, while Llaima held itself erect, with its snowy peak. Your father began to think about his time in prison. Of those terrible days after the *coup d'état*. He was obsessed by this period, I'm not telling you anything new. He saw himself standing, surrounded by fifteen other men who shared his cell. He remembered Chico Sagardia, Lalo Echeverria, Pato

Gonzalez, his colleagues and friends, whom he was seeing, within those four walls, for the last time. He was mad to be thinking back on those moments, he told me on the phone. He was there before them, he was breathing, they too were breathing, and all knew that some of them would never come out of that jail alive. He told himself that such memories lead nowhere. Memory and imagination only exacerbate suffering, become prisons themselves. That is why, with the years, he had repressed all thoughts of that period."

Before going on, she cleared her throat again, this time as if to excuse herself for what she was going to say.

"And I don't know if you knew this, but the soldiers never let anyone go to the bathroom. Except those who were collaborating. In your father's cell, no one was collaborating. And so as the days passed, their pants soaked with urine, the smell of excrement ever stronger, some of them cracked. They became aggressive, sad, you get the idea. Lalo in particular rolled around on the ground, had fits as if he were asthmatic. It seems he was claustrophobic. But despite everything, people got along. They made a common front, and when they had to they banged their cups against the bars."

It was the first time someone had told him about his father's experience in prison. Forced for so many years to imagine this incarceration, he had ended up inventing an account that had nothing to do with what he was hearing.

"And so your father was there, his hands on the steering wheel of the pickup, and the memory came back to him of the days when he and Chico Sagardia were put in solitary confinement. You remember Chico, no? He took care of communications in the Arica hospital, when your father was director. He was his right-hand man. In the evening Chico often came to eat with us, and sometimes he brought along Yiyo his son, who went with you to the hospital daycare. You remember, don't you?"

Alberto had vague memories of all that, and he wondered whether those images were not the product of his imagination. On the other hand, he had a vivid recollection of the feelings that companioned him, constantly. A kind of shame, and a persistent chill. This was paradoxical given that Arica, the country's northernmost city, was also its hottest. It was there that he learned about deception, humiliation, and the pains of love, as when his mother found out about his father's longstanding relationship with his secretary, a volatile woman with black curly hair who bent down to Alberto to offer him a sucker as he gazed into her bottomless décolleté.

"They transferred them to windowless cells," went on his mother. "Two metres by one metre, side by side. Your father was driving faster and faster. The pickup's steering wheel was shaking in his hands. He saw again the eyes of the officer who came to check up on him through the slit in the door. His eyes were pale, steel green. He uttered the same sentence, over and over: 'And the worst is, that we think we're better than animals...' And then he moved on with a deep laugh, barely to be heard. Your father remembered that he sometimes bolted wide awake in the frigid blackness of the cell and strained his eyes, but to no purpose, the darkness was so complete. He told me that he had never spent so much time meditating on the essence, the true nature of the odour of shit. Many years later, any anus, his own, that of a baby, brought back the painful memory of the days spent in that cell, looking to death as a deliverance. And so he was there, at the wheel of his vehicle, turning this over in his mind, when he came to himself and saw, through the lowered window, the panicked appearance of his men. He slammed on the brakes, and red dust rose up in his wake like a ghostly presence."

Roberto got down from the pickup, his men drew back to let him pass, and it was then that he saw a formless shape on the ground. After long seconds, he made out the fallen calf that, God in heaven, had hurled itself against the fence's barbed wire as if it had wanted to jump over! Stunned, he stared at the blood-soaked fur of the animal, its glassy eyes, its tongue that, like a foreign body, protruded from its mouth.

"Who did that, for Christ's sake?" he asked his men, all of whom turned their heads away. And the fact that they didn't even have the courage to look him in the eyes, that they seemed not unhappy that he lose an animal, made him see red.

"Then," Carmen went on, "a boy, the youngest of the workers, stepped out from the group. He was small, moved like someone in a drunken stupor, and he wore his cap very low as if to hide the fact that he was cross-eyed."

Roberto approached the boy, looked him up and down, and into his mind came the officer's eyes, bright as a razor blade. At once he froze, because he thought he had buried those memories forever. He saw himself again, on his hands and knees in the cell. No, never again, he had said, between two sobs. I promise, I swear. But the officer insisted, he wanted the names of those who, in protest, after the *coup d'état*, had pillaged the hospital. The problem was that he had known nothing about this assault, nor the names of the individuals involved. I don't know anything, I swear. And the officer: Watch it, that's a bit too much swearing for my tastes. My experience has taught me that liars love to swear. You want us to start in again, with the cigarettes? A calculated laugh then, quickly cut short. You know, I'm counting on you. It was you or Sagardia. And Sagardia, well, now he's just rotten meat... And in fact, for two hours, or three, or even four, there had been no sound at all from the neighbouring cell. Utter silence. When he came to his senses, the boy at his feet was squirming like a worm, spitting blood. Around him, men were staring at him, horrified, while others had lowered their heads or were wiping their brows with the backs of their wrists. And behind the boy, there was still the dead animal's glistening, wide-open eye.

74

"The boy was hospitalized immediately," said Carmen. "He lay in bed for ten days. Then," she added, almost inaudibly, "he died."

Alberto didn't immediately feel the blow.

"I wish I could tell you that it's all a hideous joke," she said.

He looked at his mother's sunken cheeks and saw her angry demeanour. He was astounded that, despite all his father had put her through, she could still muster some sympathy for him.

In a voice that seemed to have travelled an enormous distance, she went on with her story. And Alberto had no trouble at all imagining his father, an autumn evening, enjoying a cigarette on a garden chair. He was so exhausted, so sore after his hard day, that he didn't even take notice of the persistent wind that was making him shiver. Diego, at his feet, rose up to sniff the air and began barking angrily. Three silhouettes, outlined against the bright sky, were coming straight towards them, machetes in hand. His father stood, seized the shotgun that never left his side. He took his time aiming and pressed the trigger. The bullet buried itself in the earth just short of the men's boots. He heard the insults that issued forth. Everything you could think of, his whore of a mother, his balls, his anus. They swore to their gods on high that they would avenge the boy. Roberto lowered the shotgun, spat to the side, and offered himself the luxury of turning his back on them as he sat back down.

"A few weeks later," Carmen said, "a policeman came to the farm."

Opening the door, Roberto saw a youth dressed in a khaki shirt and brown pants. Noting the small eucalyptus trees in staggered rows on a sloping parcel of land, the young man, to make conversation, enquired after that year's planting. On his arrival, you see, that stand of trees had caught his attention, and it took him right back to his own childhood. His father cultivated the same tree near Lican Ray. You might not believe this, he said, lowering his voice, but as I was coming along the little road next to the Mapuche settlement, two *indios*, at least that's what they looked like, tried to bar my way. No, but who do they think they are? Soon they'll be claiming that Araucania still belongs to them! And he burst out laughing. He took his time before getting around to the death of the boy, and when at last he broached the subject, Roberto saw that he was uneasy about the whole business.

"It seems," said Carmen, "that he really was young. He talked freely, and he talked a lot."

The policeman turned solemn and formal when he had to ask him for his version of the facts concerning the boy, whom he named only once. Roberto complied. He was driving his pickup, got down from his vehicle, the young worker was pushing the calf towards the barbed wire, and seeing Roberto, he came at him with a knife in his hand. Roberto had to defend himself. All through this brief account the policeman nodded his head vigorously, hastening to set everything down in a notebook, as if the sooner he preserved this version, the sooner he recorded it, then the sooner that stream of images and fantastical impressions would supplant what was real. When Roberto had finished, the policeman, to conclude, said: "That's what we thought, self-defence."

It all lasted just a few minutes. When he left, the officer touched his fingers to the visor of his cap, and turned about with the same alertness he had displayed all through the interview.

"Believe it or not," said Carmen, "your father was never given any trouble in the wake of that affair. Of course, the workers, mostly Mapuches, never treated him the same way afterwards. No more bantering. They talked to him just when they had to. Several times your father surprised them plotting against him. He waited, waited for them to sabotage his equipment, to kill his animals or to set them loose, and he was ready to defend himself, but nothing happened."

Alberto remained thoughtful.

"How long after the boy's death did he meet Amalia?" he asked her.

"A year, a year and a half."

"And how did he manage to get through it all? After all, he'd killed somebody," he added, lowering his voice.

"He phoned me, told me about his nightmares, where he was stretched out on a mountain of bones. Where he tried to get up and couldn't. I said to him, sorry, but for someone who's spent his whole life denying his Jewishness, that's rather ironic. It's a Jewish dream. And he answered, you're right. And it's funny you should say that, because the older I get, the more I'm like the old man, and to tell you the truth, that terrifies me."

Once again, Alberto was struck by the compassion in his mother's voice. He said to himself: she always loved him.

Later, as a hint of light began to creep in behind the blinds, they shared memories of his father as a thoughtful and teasing husband, as a man acting according to his convictions. A smile brightened the face of his mother when he spoke of his childhood picture of his father: a man with a fierce smile, who, despite his modest height, was larger than life size. They spent a good hour exchanging stories, recalling humorous incidents, sometimes from Chile, sometimes from Quebec, where his father was always in the thick of the action, showing off, before the eyes wide with amazement of his Quebec friends, a pike almost a metre long, or wearing a bullet-proof vest destined for a guerrilla in the capital, and passing through Chilean customs in the middle of the 1980s, when he was still *persona non grata* in the country. Luckily, he was let off easy by a customs official who, like him, was from the South. His father, Alberto ventured, was the only one in the family who could have been a character out of a novel. To the point where, when he was recounting one of his exploits, his friends were frankly incredulous, assuming he

78

exaggerated out of self-regard. But as he and his mother talked, the picture darkened, and the debonair, lively, and smiling man turned into one who was Machiavellian, wounded, and cunning. And once this second image had supplanted the first, Carmen, her voice hoarse, was unequivocal:

"For me, and I always said so, it was the *coup d'état* that spoiled everything. After that, he was never the same."

6

The next morning Alberto was driving along Avenida Caupolicán at thirty kilometres an hour, following the hearse. The sun's rays pierced the clouds and shone down between two automobiles onto the polished surface of a glass building in the middle of a vacant lot, where clumps of grass grew between cement blocks. On the horizon, the fog's woolly vapours had decapitated Mount Ñielol. On the south slope of the mountain, between the silvered lindens whose leaves shone like mirrors, he saw warlike Mapuche totems covered in white blotches (bird excrement? graffiti?). When he felt his forehead, his fingers came away covered in perspiration.

Stopped at an intersection, Alberto saw his son in the rear-view mirror, wide-eyed, staring at a cart. The man atop the vehicle wore a poncho and held himself erect, holding the reins of an old horse with a glossy hide. Suddenly the cart, the man's dress, and his expression of artless arrogance seemed like a violent intrusion out of the past. Farther on, when he entered the Avenida Balmaceda, he found himself in another world, where the aromas of coriander and garlic held sway, and where the Mapuche women, all dressed in black with scarves on their heads, sold tomatoes, lettuce, carrots, huge onions, and all sorts of pumpkins behind makeshift stands, but also *merquén, nalcas*, and *digüeñes*. And Alberto remembered coming to the *feria* with his grandparents, holding his Abuela's hand and watching his Abuelo stride a few metres ahead, pick up a cherimoya fruit, and smell its skin for a long time before driving a hard bargain for half a dozen.

Beside him, wearing dark glasses, his mother was inscrutable, as if she was tired of exposing her vulnerability. Through the outside rear-view mirror he saw Noemi's red Nissan and Gabriel's black Impala. To think that, of his father's dozen brothers and sisters, only three had come to his funeral. He remembered what Araya had said: "Your father didn't know how to make himself loved."

He passed through the wrought iron gate of the cemetery. Above the arch formed by the branches of oak he saw a shifting grey sky that reminded him of a vast radioactive cloud. The sunlight was muted, white and diffuse. Mechanically, he parked in front of the mound where the ceremony would take place, and where the rabbi, wearing a black tunic, was already pacing back and forth, an open Bible in his hand, rehearsing, it would seem, the selections he would read. Alberto circled the car, breathing in the heavy and humid air, and helped Marco to get down. Along with his mother and his son, he advanced to greet his Abuela, installed in a wheelchair, then Noemi, Hannah, and Gabriel. On everyone's face, other than that of his Abuela, there was deep sorrow, despondency at not being able to escape the oppressive atmosphere. Seeing that the others felt as he did gave him some comfort. Holding his son's hand, he made his way towards the hill surrounded by weeping willows.

Some sturdy, tanned men in shirtsleeves appeared with the coffin. Their brusque manner, their cold eyes, greatly irritated Alberto. Their careless demeanour suggested this was a poor-paying job. He clutched his son's hand more tightly, and Marco sought his eyes. He tried to concentrate on the undulation of the willow leaves. That calmed him for a moment, but he was beset by visions. A moonlit night, dark silhouettes coming on in haste. Stopping in front of his father and himself, forming a compact mass, like an outcropping whose crest was lit. Mist rose from their bodies. The solitary howl of a wolf broke the night's silence. Suddenly, large heavy hands were beating down on them. The blows were dull, the pain numbing. The rest was a relentless moving blur. Then he saw the glint of a blade, a kitchen knife …

Supported by ropes in the hands of men in shirtsleeves, the coffin was lowered jerkily into the grave. The rabbi read the Holy Book with darting eyes. He compared the body to a piece of fabric, and the soul, eternal and inviolable, to a bird taking flight on a spring morning such as this, setting its eyes on each person present, one by one. And at once, as if Alberto had just received a violent blow to his back, everything misted over. The arching branches, the vaporous grey sky, the penitent silhouettes surrounding him, that was perhaps what the end of the world was like. He saw his son, his small arms holding onto his thigh, saw the tender compassion on his angelic face. Then he felt the warm hand of his mother on his cheek.

Towards the end of the ceremony, as he was pulling himself together, he spotted in the distance, near the gate, a young woman and a short man, side by side, their wrists crossed low over their bodies, watching them. When Noemi went towards them and signalled them to come nearer, the woman shook her head no. Seeing that Noemi continued to approach, she turned about as if frightened, and left the cemetery with the old man at her heels, head lowered, not looking back. At first Alberto was so disconcerted that he did not make the connection with the portraits Noemi had sketched for him. Two days later he bitterly reproached himself for not having guessed that it was Amalia and her father.

All of a sudden it came back to him that the Ventura burial site was located in front of a fountain, in the southern sector, at the other end of the cemetery, where ordinarily two Mapuche women stood selling bouquets. What did that mean?

"Why wasn't he buried with Abuelo?" he asked, approaching Noemi.

All heads turned in his direction.

"We can't do this. Why did no one tell me?"

"I tried my best to convince the others. But they didn't want to listen."

And so, as the rabbi's monotone continued its litany, he took Marco's hand and walked away. He heard, over the noise of his feet on the gravel, Noemi's voice imploring him to come back. His blood was pounding in his temples, the path reeled before him. As he was settling Marco onto the rear seat, his mother appeared at his side and opened the passenger door. When he started the engine, he glimpsed Noemi, who raised her arm to him, her face haggard. He backed up the truck and drove along the high fence looking for the exit.

WHEN HE LET HIS MOTHER off at his Aunt Emma's, he was grateful to her for keeping Marco without asking any questions. As they were embracing on the sidewalk, he saw his uncle Pedro at the top of the steps, his moustache drooping, his expression betraying a desire to impose an authority he had lost long ago. He got back into the pickup and took off.

Rapidly, he drove out of the city. Following an interminable alley of poplars, he thought about his father lying on his back on a winter night. The road climbed and descended, abruptly and unpredictably. *Campesinos* walked along, heads bowed, long stripped branches over their shoulders, followed by two oxen held side by side by a rudimentary yoke over their heads. Soon he passed a series of impressive *fundos*: in front of meticulously painted

85

fences and houses, horses grazed in closed paddocks built just for them, and children, wearing twill overalls, played in yards also designed for them, where everything was imbued with a kind of happiness that deserved to be put on display. Farther on, beyond a steep hill, he came upon another world, ruled by a different code: narrow plots of land appeared, where diminutive housewives in white aprons were hanging up threadbare laundry, while behind them, as if a cyclone had recently passed over the property, there was a confusion of broken toys and wooden sheds turned grey by the constant assault of wind and rain.

At the end of a long stretch of straight road bordered by bushes and apple trees scattered across a valley extending to the foot of a fogbound range of the Andes, a green sign announced the town of Cunco. It bordered the great agricultural properties owned by the old Basque latifundium families (*Etcheverry*, *Duhart*, *Etchepare*, one read on the rough wood panels), properties that, as far as the eye could see, boasted fields of corn and oats. Shortly before he came to the town itself, the hills flattened abruptly to become a kind of false plain that petered out when here and there the first little bungalows appeared, then the city hall, a wine-red colonial house. Under a niggardly sun, he drove slowly so as to take in the façades of the buildings on both sides of the street. Passersby kept crossing in the middle of the road, their silhouettes mirrored on the hood of the vehicle, while, even with the windows up, the cries of the itinerant peddlers reached him distinctly.

He passed in front of Plaza de Armas where the bottoms of the tree trunks were painted bottle green, just like the surrounding benches, and where the tops, to the height of a six-foot man, were gleaming white, like the fountain. Students talked together on the grass, while others strolled on the promenade. At one intersection there was a group of straw-hatted men, very likely Mapuches, all standing with one foot propped against the wall of a grocery store.

As soon as he saw a sign with two crossed guns on a green background, the symbol for the national police, he parked the pickup. He crossed the street diagonally, circled the stalls overflowing with lemons and coriander, and arrived in front of the narrow façade, painted khaki, just like the policemen's shirts. He climbed the stairs leading to the entrance, and once inside found himself facing a man in uniform. He had pink cheeks, and the stool on which he sat was a good distance from the counter, due to his ample girth.

Without looking up, the officer asked him what he could do for him. To his chagrin, Alberto became tongue-tied as he was trying to explain. To make himself clear, he repeated:

"I want to see the police report on the death of Roberto Ventura."

Puffing out his cheeks, the man replied, indifferent:

"Identification."

When the officer saw his Canadian passport and identification papers, his defiance gave way to a naïve curiosity. He leafed through the passport, turned it over several times, seemed very interested by it. Several times he looked up furtively from the papers to Alberto's face. How many days had he been in Chile? Why did he so much want to see this report?

"Is that a joke? My father is dead. He-is-dead! I have a right to see the report!"

The man held his gaze for a long time. Casually, he got up and walked away, past the desks where secretaries and other policemen were sitting. No heads were raised as he passed. At the far end of the room, lit by rectangular fluorescent fixtures, he stopped to lean over a muscular man at a typewriter. He whispered in his ear, and after a moment the muscular individual glanced over at Alberto, then discreetly shook his head no. There was a short exchange, and the officer strolled back, as casually as he had left. Laboriously, he sat himself back down on the stool, pretended to look for something on the counter, then at last jerked his chin vaguely towards the chairs behind Alberto. He then leaned his entire body weight on his elbow, and exhaled noisily.

Reluctantly, Alberto went to sit down.

Three times, he got up to see whether the muscled man was still behind his typewriter, and each time the officer gave him a baleful look. Alberto sighed repeatedly. Seeing him, the officer got up and went back to his colleague. There was another quiet discussion, and after a few moments, the policeman came back to the counter.

"You're out of luck. He's too busy today."

Alberto was reaching the boiling point. The man continued to stare at him.

Suddenly, out of nowhere, the officer turned, stuck two fingers in his mouth, and whistled in the direction of the burly individual, who at that moment was holding his phone between his neck and chin. A few heads turned in the room, and looked towards the counter. The muscleman also raised his eyes. When he hung up and came towards Alberto, it became clear that his physique was even more impressive than he had imagined. He leaned his two large hands on the counter, and scowled.

He was young, very young to be a lieutenant. His eyes were large, black, and a bit slanted; his nose, generous. His face seemed gentle.

Calmly, Alberto repeated that he wanted to read the police report.

"What do you want to verify?"

"I've a right to see this report. Will you please bring it to me!"

The lieutenant fixed him with his eyes for a long time then began to laugh.

"It's not what you think. You're mistaken, my friend," he said. "It's not at all what you think."

His laughing eyes scanned the room, as he savoured the silence that had returned. He lowered his head, and without looking at him, said a bit more softly:

"I'm on your side."

Alberto studied his body language; it was as if he were behaving like an old friend in a bar, sharing in his disappointments.

"This report won't tell you anything," said the lieutenant, almost whispering. "It's nothing at all, this report."

And he lowered his head a bit, as if to signal that he was making a compromising admission. Alberto heard the words clearly, but it took a number of seconds for him to absorb their meaning.

The lieutenant turned towards the officer at the counter, and gave him a sign with his head. Slowly, the officer walked over to a metal filing cabinet, opened a drawer, and pulled out a file. He came back with the document and placed it on the counter. Alberto opened the folder, and with the lieutenant looking on, began reading the report. He was soon disappointed. Noemi had been right: the document was extremely brief, containing, on the first page, only some factual information to identify his father, while the second page concluded in three lines that there was "internal bleeding," hypothesizing a "wound" inflicted while working on the farm. Not a word about the scar on his side. No autopsy.

"Do you want a copy?" the lieutenant asked.

Without waiting for an answer, the lieutenant signalled his colleague, who went to the photocopier. The officer came back with the document, which he held out to Alberto.

"Why do you say that it's nothing at all, this report?" asked Alberto, searching the lieutenant's eyes.

The lieutenant smiled, half amused, half ill at ease. He was like a bright, innocent boy. He lifted the movable section of the counter, lowered it noiselessly, and passed in front of the chairs. Alberto thought he heard him say "follow me," and saw the lieutenant already descending the stairs and opening the door, holding it ajar with his foot. He hesitated, then went after him, the report in his hand.

Outside, as they walked rapidly side by side through the pedestrian traffic, they were assaulted by a cacophony of honking horns, cries, and roaring engines.

Looking straight ahead, as if seeking someone in the crowd, the lieutenant said, as if he were thinking out loud:

"I had a feeling this business was going to crop up again. I didn't know when or how, but I knew it. To tell you the truth, it's even given me nightmares. But I can tell you one thing: you surprised me. I didn't know that Don Roberto had a son in Canada. It appears," he said, smiling, "that no one thought to tell me…"

Trying to keep up with him, Alberto bumped into an old lady who stopped, furious, and followed him with her dark eyes.

"But tell me," Alberto asked, "there's something else, right?"

Suddenly the lieutenant stopped cold and held out his hand to an old man in a black beret who was sitting cross-legged on a wooden box near a newspaper stand, enjoying a cigarette. His eyes sleepy and grey, the old man responded with a limp handshake. After a preamble that was virtually incomprehensible to Alberto because of the old man's unorthodox pronunciation, he said that the "activity" was as slow as it had ever been, but there was no reason to worry because it would pick up just like last year over the summer. For now, if truth be told, the guys were taking it easy... Without waiting for the old man to finish his assessment, the lieutenant turned towards Alberto to say:

"They destroyed him."

Alberto froze.

"What? Who, 'they'?"

The lieutenant began walking a bit faster, while leaning towards Alberto:

"You don't know how we do things, do you? It's obvious that you're not from around here. Your father had no luck, he died at a very bad time. Right away his case went political. Wait for me here."

The lieutenant disappeared into the crowded grocery store, long and narrow, that Alberto had noticed before. It smelled of paprika, cider, and grilled meat. Alberto realized that all the men there were native, then he read the slogans on the walls: *Para una nación mapuche libre; Autonomía y respeto de los pueblos indígenas de Chile*... Most of the men held a tract in their hands. The lieutenant tried to push his way through, but the men, without moving, turned their backs on him as if to block his way. Seeing the lieutenant

92

in the middle of these men, everything became clear, and he reproached himself for not having understood earlier: he was a Mapuche. The lieutenant shoved somebody, who lost his balance. The men around him gave way finally, but their eyes were threatening. Like a cock prepared to defend himself, the lieutenant cast hostile glances in all directions. He found himself nose to nose, at the very back of the store, with a bald man wearing a scarf around his neck and holding a microphone. The man stopped talking. The lieutenant grabbed the mike out of his hand and proclaimed, his voice echoing: "This meeting is illegal!" There was a paralyzing silence. Then the crowd started to murmur, became restless. Arms reached towards the lieutenant, hands tried, it seemed, to topple him. But, agile, the lieutenant blocked the blows, and freed himself to glare about him defiantly. He ordered the people to disperse. At first no one moved, then, after seconds had passed, the Mapuches shuffled, reluctantly, towards the exit. The lieutenant rejoined Alberto, still on the sidewalk, and they went off together. Once they had gone a good ten metres, they distinctly heard behind them:

"You're not ashamed, *chuchetumadre*... One day you'll get what you deserve, you piece of shit..."

His eyes half closed, the lieutenant pretended not to hear. Only twenty metres later, he said:

"You saw? Now you know what I'm trying to say? They're all parasites. That's what it amounts to, their ancestral philosophy: to get everything for nothing."

"Tell me, have you been to my father's farm, where one of his workers died?"

The lieutenant nodded yes, following a truck with his eyes, where propane canisters were banging against each other.

"And the autopsy?"

The lieutenant greeted a woman on the other side of the street, who was stirring *sopaipillas* frying in oil that gave off black smoke.

"What?"

They looked at each other nervously.

"Why was there nothing in the report about my father's scar?"

The lieutenant first became pensive, and then, as though he'd had enough of this discussion, and as if to get rid of him as quickly as possible, he said all in one breath:

"Listen, I can't tell you everything, or I'm finished. Why should all this fall on me? I don't know you, I have a family to feed ... With what they did to your father, we had the goods on them. We go to court, we win. This business, excuse me, was a gift from heaven for us. And then ... the mayor of Cunco decided to support Huenchumilla ... do I have to say more?"

A white truck came to a stop in front of the square, its brakes exhaling slowly.

"Ever since, Huenchumilla and our mayor have been like that," he said, crossing his index and middle fingers. "As soon as Huenchumilla was told about the affair, he asked for it to be hushed up. You know, a Mapuche politician who is trying to get elected, with a sordid murder in the background involving native people... I can tell you that I'll never forget those two guys from City Hall who came to the station one afternoon. They asked us to leave, and the next day, when we opened the office, there was no trace of the report on your father... I tell you, this story makes me sick."

"Why did you say murder?"

"Sorry, but that's all you're going to get out of me. I've already said too much, my friend."

For a moment, the lieutenant seemed to feel for him, as if it had just occurred to him that the revelations he'd made might have been hurtful. He turned his back on Alberto and lost himself in the noisy crowd. Ten metres on, he was jogging back to the police station.

Clouds curled around each other, promiscuous, overhead, as Alberto wandered among beggars holding out creased palms and women with masculine faces who stared at him shamelessly. He was convinced that they all knew he was not from there. Even the youngest, it seemed, turned as he passed to follow him for two, three, four seconds, with disdainful curiosity.

He crossed the street without looking. A driver honked furiously, but Alberto didn't react. He wanted to escape the promiscuity, the invasive scrutiny, but wherever he turned he stumbled on someone who followed him avidly with his eyes. He walked on, left the Plaza de Armas behind him, and, passing a group of women sitting cross-legged on the ground, he raised his eyes to the tops of the furry araucarias, behind which rose the Llaima volcano, perpetually snow-topped, serene, as if what went on down below did not concern it.

Soon he found himself on a quiet street, bordered by small houses with puny gardens. A man with greying temples and carefully combed hair looked at him suspiciously. He was leaning on a cane, and for a good long time he didn't move a finger.

"Yes?" asked Alberto, going up to him, "Can I help you?"

The man spat on the ground, pulled out a handkerchief to wipe his lips, and turned his back on him before slowly heading home.

Alberto stood there, his arms hanging by his side, his breathing shallow.

At the end of this same street, he stopped before a white building with horizontal lines, where students in uniform (blue blazers, grey flannel pants, white shirts) sat talking on benches or standing in front of a dirt path. The carefree exuberance of the young people was hard for him to watch. Now that he found himself in the small town where his father grew up, in the place where (at least in his imagination) everything began, he felt like a foreigner, someone from the West who is fleeing his dreary life, and who has lost his bearings.

But… was this not his father's school? The asphalt yard was empty, and seemed inordinately large. After a moment, as he was watching, he saw a lone adolescent appear, small, his hair cut short on the sides but curly on top, walking confidently, a blue blazer slung over his shoulder. The boy bent his knees, his face thin, browned by the sun, his body seemingly weightless. He walked but he did not advance, he appeared to levitate, eclipsing everything around him.

On the other side of the street, there was a crowd. It had converged on what seemed to be a restaurant: *La Mesa de los Sueños*.

Inside, voices reverberated, deafening him. From time to time peals of laughter erupted, glasses banged together. They were mostly students, four or five together around square tables.

When a stool came free at the counter, Alberto sat down. He looked at the menu and finally ordered, like his neighbour, a breaded pork chop, mashed potatoes, and a glass of red wine. Behind the counter, two young men his age came and went, sometimes pulling a beer out of the refrigerator, sometimes plunging dishes into the sink. Alberto ate slowly, not so much to savour the food as to gather his thoughts. He could not believe it, it seemed too absurd, too unreal. *His father had been murdered...* He looked around him: life went on, sardonic and unchanging.

He put down a few bills to pay for his meal. He stood up, skirted the counter, and, not knowing quite why, turned his head towards the mirror behind the bar, where there was a multitude of bottles. The black and white photograph was taped to the mirror, a bit crooked, its corners worn. Not believing his eyes, he rested his hands on the counter to lean in closer. Yes, it was the very same photo he had seen in one of the family albums. Four young men, in jacket and tie, arms linked, smiling widely, their eyes half-closed. The third from the left was his father. He was seventeen, eighteen at the most. Bright dots where his eyes should be, his face shining, he smiled, looking tired but tough. It was his father through and through, his father the tightrope walker.

"Did you recognize someone?" asked one of the young men behind the counter, as he was shining a glass.

His head shaved, wide-shouldered, he sported a two- or three-day-old beard that covered his face right to the cheekbones.

"That's my father," said Alberto.

The young man looked at the photograph.

"You're Roberto's son?"

Radiant, the young man put the glass and towel down on the counter, and stretched out his hand. Then, as if suddenly ashamed of his reserve, he embraced him over the counter, whispering in his ear: "All my sympathies, my friend," and held him close for a long time. His name was Pablo. In a resonant voice, speaking quickly, he explained that he was the son of Raúl, the owner of the restaurant, second from the left in the photograph, with the frizzy hair and the round face. Was this the same Raúl who, according to Noemi, had found his father's body?

"When they were young, they were like brothers. You know this photo, no?"

They began to talk about the dance that had become legendary with time, and suddenly Alberto felt as if these were characters out of a cult film. They were euphoric, they had finished their years at the lycée, and would soon, for the most part, be going on to university. On the other hand, they had to say goodbye to a whole world with its pranks, its open-hearted companionship, it extravagant dreams, and its at times salutary childishness. Pablo told him that the two others in the photo had also died. One, who had become a member of the Revolutionary Left during the dictatorship, disappeared, probably dropped from a helicopter somewhere off the coast, near Puerto Saavedra. The other died of heart failure ten or so years previously. Nostalgic, and gently ironic, as if looking back on their own youth, they launched into a discussion of idealism and the need to stay rebellious at heart.

It appeared that since Roberto's return to the region, since he had taken over his father's land, which adjoined that of Pablo's parents, the two friends had connected again, and had begun working together. Roberto rented his friend's equipment, chainsaws, cranes, tractors, to clear the fields on his land. He then sold the wood to Araucania Madera, the forestry industry giant for the area. When Alberto told Pablo what had led him to Cunco, Pablo said he knew very little about what had happened.

"You should go to see my father. I think he'd have things to tell you. But, how should I say this? He's not been right for some years, he's become bitter with age ..."

He promised to alert his parents to his visit, and told him how to get to the village of Las Violetas. When Alberto got up to go, Pablo embraced him for a long time as if they were old friends, and wished him luck.

HERE AND THERE, Alberto spotted hares that leaped up, only to disappear in puffy clouds of dust. Along the road, bushes dotted with small flowers hibernated under a coat of dirt. Several times, the pickup's chassis struck a stone on the ground. Twice, going uphill, he had to shift into second gear.

As he climbed a steep slope, then skirted a house with a dish antenna, he kept his eyes peeled for the Star of David, and found it hanging from an oak beside the road at the entrance to Las Violetas. The seven or eight houses that made up the village, whose families were mostly Jewish, were all perched over a small valley that provided a matchless view of Llaima and the land around, and were so widely spaced that they seemed not to belong together.

Jolting along, he passed hectares and hectares of cleared land that made him think of a battlefield. He only saw the white house with tiles once he reached the farm's gate. He stopped the vehicle, got down without turning off the engine, and as he went to open the gate, was assailed by the odour of eucalyptus. It was pleasant at first, then insistent and dizzying.

Slowly, avoiding the depressions, he navigated the road leading to the farm, bordered by spindly bushes. All over the property there were pails, gas canisters, fences whose pickets were lying in the tall grass. He parked the vehicle in front of the house, close to a kennel.

He saw that the door was half open, and that the handle had been forced. A chair was overturned in the middle of the living room, the television stand had been stripped of its TV set, and there were mud prints on the floor. On the right, the kitchen cupboards and drawers were open.

The other rooms were in the same state of disorder.

He emerged as the evening drew out its last beams of light. From the porch, the prospect was staggering: a huge swathe of his father's land had been reduced to an expanse of mud, a jumble of dead branches, zones of dying grass, trunks chopped into shavings. It reminded him of the picture books he'd leafed through as a child, those books that fascinated him so, where one saw soldiers huddled in trenches surrounded by barbed wire, their eyes shining with a dead light, their faces expressionless. But what did it all mean? Had his father done that? He who all his life had shown more respect for nature than for the men and women around him? Countless questions filled his mind, sinister questions with no answers, and he began to experience the same sense of loss, irremediable loss, that he had often felt as an adolescent after an argument with his father.

Farther on still, yesterday's patchwork of cultivated land had given way to an ocean of eucalyptus, extending from Las Violetas to the Cunco steeple. He thought about his father, who, as a child, covered the ground on bare feet between the family house and school, his shoes tied around his neck so as not to wear them out. Today, he thought, it would be impossible to cut through that dense forest. And then, in the distance, unchanging and unreal in the orange light, Llaima. A bit to the side, between two hills, a cluster of straw huts and small houses poorly aligned. That's where they live, he thought, scanning the village.

He decided to put some order into the house.

When he had finished, he stretched out on the couch.

He turned over and over for a long time, wondering what he should do. When night fell he could not shut his eyes, anxious as he was: what did he want to know, finally? Was he not wasting his time? What good would it do to prove that his father had been murdered? Was he putting his own life in danger by staying in his father's house? How would the murderers react when they learned that he was roaming about trying to shed light on what happened, to shed light on it all? And damn, he should have been more open with his mother and his son ...

WHEN HE OPENED HIS EYES, he was blinded by the sun.

He got up. There was water he could drink, but no electricity. He found coffee, eggs, kosher salted crackers. In Montreal, as these crackers were found everywhere, his father began to buy them; it was as if they were the only link he allowed himself to maintain with the Jewish religion. But then right away he remembered the story his father told to his brother and himself, around a campfire, in a car, or the rare times he put them to bed. As his father changed the names of the characters, it was only years later that he learned that it was all about the prophet Jeremiah.

He ate fried eggs standing up in front of the kitchen counter, then he sipped his coffee on the porch while looking out on the dew, which, like an enormous silk cloak fallen from the sky, covered the grass, the hillocks of earth, the flowers, the pickup, Diego's kennel (but what had happened to the stray dog that had won his father's approval?).

In Egypt, trying to allay the discontent of his people in exile, Jeremiah counselled resignation. One could, said the prophet, be perfectly happy outside holy ground, if one saw to one's relationship with Yahweh. Jeremiah was an idealist, and most Jews of his time saw him as a traitor. What was it that drew his father to this story, he who advocated the exact opposite? Who never missed an opportunity to contend that one could not be happy outside one's native land? Being an immigrant was an abomination, it forced you to abide by your status as a second-class citizen. Perhaps, deep down, his father was unsure of his convictions, and Jeremiah's argument held more sway with him than he wanted to admit.

Going through the closet in his father's bedroom, he found a shotgun. He examined it; it was not loaded. He found the cartridges in a kitchen drawer. Outside, behind the house, he aimed at the trunk of a eucalyptus tree. The gun went off, but as his arm cushioned the shock poorly, the bullet lost itself in the greenery. The report, exaggerated, dramatic, set his left ear to ringing. He reloaded the shotgun and balanced an empty gas can on a fence post. As he was holding his breath and aiming, he heard a man's voice:

"Hey, what are you up to? We thought you'd be here..."

He turned towards the man without noticing that he was pointing his gun at him. His Uncle Pedro bent down, raising his hand.

"Hey! What's going on?"

Alberto didn't move, just looked at him.

"Don't point that at me, I tell you!"

Alberto lowered the weapon.

"What's got into you? Have you gone crazy, or what?"

His uncle looked him up and down.

"Go on, get your stuff. This farce has gone on long enough."

Gun in hand, Alberto stared back, impassive.

"Go on, I said," repeated his uncle, gesturing with his head. "I'll wait for you."

"You're wasting your time. I'm not going anywhere."

"What? Look, I promised your mother that I'd bring you back, and I'm going to keep my word, believe me."

With his gun, Alberto indicated that he should leave.

"Where do you think you are? In a Western? This is real life here, *macoso!* You see those houses down there," he said, turning around. "You see those *rucas* down there? That's where they live, the Mapus. When they find out that you're here all by yourself, what do you think they're going to do? Bring you a welcome present, maybe?"

He had a little forced laugh that Alberto found familiar.

"For the last time, I'm asking you to leave, *tio.*"

His uncle stood there, open-mouthed.

"I promised your mother. And you know me, I'm a man of my word."

Alberto went towards him, slowly. They were about the same build, but his uncle had aged terribly. His seventy years weighed on him. Before, he had been a tough customer, who didn't hesitate to use his fists when he thought he had to. But the menial jobs he had to do all his life, in the lumber industry, in Chile and in Canada, had bent his back, whitened his hair, shrunk his features. It was his parents who had sponsored his aunt and uncle so they could immigrate to Quebec. Not long after they arrived in Montreal, it was inevitable, Pedro and his father fell out over something trivial on Christmas Day. The picture of his father, one knee on his uncle's chest, his fist in the air, ready to disfigure him, against a background of twinkling, multicoloured Christmas tree lights, was imprinted on his memory. As of then, his father had become *persona non grata* on the maternal side of Alberto's family.

"But what's happened to you?" asked Pedro. "What did we do to you? Okay, your father's left us, but you don't have to lose your mind because of that. Alberto, Albertito, *escúchame*. It's good to want to know the truth. There, you're right. But there are people for that. And can we talk frankly for two seconds? All that for your father?"

Pedro hinted at a nervous smile.

"You know, you and I, it's true, we never clicked. What do you want, sometimes it's like that between men," he said, shrugging his shoulders.

He paused, as though to gauge the impact of his words.

"But what I've never forgiven you, is to have fallen into your father's trap. Just like Carmen. You know how I love and respect your mother, no? When your grandmother died," he said, referring to a time that he never missed a chance to resurrect, "it was Emma and I who took care of her and saw to her education. Working hard, sometimes day and night. But the way your mother worshipped your father, she knew what I thought about that. And I didn't mince words. And you, too, I'm sorry to say it, you fell into his trap. Not like your brother, who had the smart idea of getting away from that man, all the way to Brazil. *Putamadre*, but what did you see in him? Why waste your time looking into the death of a man who spent his whole life humiliating you?"

Alberto was seething, didn't know what to say.

"The truth is that your father was a horrible man. A man with no morals. And you want to know what his problem was? For him, there was nothing in life that was sacred. Not your mother, not your brother, not you. Not his work, nothing. The only thing that counted was him. Him and only him."

Pedro shook his head, as if to say that there were no words to describe Roberto's behaviour.

"If you want to know what's really a surprise, it's that he didn't end up like that ten, twenty years ago. That's the miracle! Because your father was a hopeless egotist, a dangerous man. Wake up, for God's sake!"

It was then that Alberto raised the shotgun, the barrel towards the sky, and before he had time to press the trigger, Pedro said in one breath:

"Okay, okay, I get it, you don't want to know. That's your right. But let me just tell you one thing. Okay? If you want me to leave after that, I'll go."

And so Alberto listened to him give chapter and verse on his father's amorous liaison with his secretary when Carmen was pregnant with him, a liaison that continued after his birth, to the great distress of his mother, who fell into a lengthy depression.

"My father," interrupted Alberto, "was a man of his time and of the country where he was born. That's no excuse of course, but he was neither an angel or a devil. He was an extravagant man, impulsive, but a man like many others of his generation. You know, in a family, in the end, everything comes out into the open, and what I've heard about you, at the beginning of your marriage, doesn't exactly look like the behaviour of a choirboy."

Pedro stared back at him without blinking.

"What are you trying to do? To change the subject by slandering me?"

His uncle then began to describe the dynamics of Alberto's family, as if he'd forgotten that Alberto himself was one of the characters in the story. Alberto was soon astonished by all the details he provided. He told himself that his mother, clearly, had confided in his aunt and uncle much more than he suspected. After a few relatively innocuous anecdotes concerning his father (his temper tantrums, his rashness, his outbursts), his uncle, his voice now full of foreboding, took him back to a glacial Montreal night, when all the windows were coated in frost, in the duplex whose very memory made Alberto shut his eyes. The husky, unremitting stream of words from his uncle, his distinctive accent, both songlike and staccato, typical of the disreputable neighbourhoods of Valparaiso, the city where he had grown up, transported him into that matrimonial bedroom where electric heat struggled against the onslaught of the cold. He clearly saw, bathed in an orange light, in this room with the thick beige carpeting, his mother bedridden like a mummy. As he remembered it, a vapour inhabited the room. His mother's night table was teeming with pill bottles. This was her sanctuary. At that time, like a traitor, like a coward, Alberto was secretly planning his escape from the household. "Like a traitor, like a coward," because his father had just (for the fourth or fifth time?) left his mother. Alberto had gone to the kitchen for a glass of water, with the unavowed intention of seeing how his mother was. Having entered her room, he put the glass down on the chest of drawers and sat in the armchair, very close to his mother who, although awake, did not turn her head towards him or express any emotion. Her eyes were like those of a blind person: they settled on no point in particular, and betrayed nothing. When she finally spoke, he pretended to be surprised by her words, which, as usual, spoke of the cruelty of men, meaning males, and the pleasure they took in destroying those dear to them. But why this pleasure? He didn't reply, knowing that was his role. It comes, she said, from an unconscious desire to avenge the humiliations and suffering they themselves had endured, it comes from their being unable to see others as happy, it comes from their undying hatred of women. She fixed her opaque gaze on that of Alberto, as if to draw out the life concentrated in his eyes, as if to cling to the painful compassion, perhaps, that she saw there. Then Pedro arrived at his presumed destination, at the extravagant sum of money piled up by his father during his two decades in Montreal, a sum his mother had just learned of due to the stupid error of a bank employee ("Excuse me, Mrs. Ventura. Truly. We were sure you were aware of the existence of this account..."). That, to his considerable surprise (since he had never heard anything about a secret bank account), was what his uncle told him.

Pedro said no more, but Alberto knew the rest. All it took was a telephone call from his father for his mother to join him in Santiago, just one call. How to talk about that, because you cannot reasonably go on calling it love. And then, one hot morning, without warning, some ten months later, he abandoned her for good, and went to live in the South.

Pedro was a few steps away, frowning. A light wind stirred his white Clark Gable toupee. He was downcast now, and Alberto could see it. But having heard enough he turned his back and went into the house. When, after a short time, he heard cawing, he glanced out the window: his uncle had disappeared. And so Alberto feasted his eyes, as his father had so often done, on the dramatic glow of the sunset, and when he raised them he saw (God in heaven, was he hallucinating?) Llaima emitting a delicate wisp of grey smoke in the form of a question mark.

8

That night, surrounded by chirping crickets, he walked up the path to the road. The flashlight's cone of light made the least irregularity, the smallest bush, seem threatening. When he heard dead branches cracking, or a rustling of leaves, he clutched his rifle butt more tightly, and strangely, that made him feel better.

On the horizon, the starless sky was as dark as the surrounding landscape. Far off he spotted, partly obscured by branches, the lit windows of a house. He came down a hill, and as he skirted the house's property, barking echoed in the night. When he stopped in front of the little aluminum gate, two large dogs, one black and one brown, entered into the cone of light, yapping, showing their fangs, and leaning their paws on the wire fencing.

A light went on on each side of the door. A woman's silhouette appeared. She called the dogs, who instantly obeyed, disappearing into the darkness. Soon all that was heard was their spasmodic breathing. The woman, whom Alberto couldn't see, asked who was there. When Alberto showed himself she approached him, smiling, her face cross-hatched with deep wrinkles, which she tolerated, one would say, stoically. Her hair, coarse as straw, colourless, fell onto her pale and ravaged cheeks. She opened the gate's latch, and said to him: "How glad I am that you've come! Come in, it's so cold."

As he negotiated the winding flat-stoned path, Alberto made out, twenty or so metres away, a large shed. Was he dreaming, or did he really see, between the bushes, through the half-open door, cranes and agricultural machinery, stored every which way? Discreetly, before entering, he left the firearm between two ferns.

The woman offered him one of the two living room couches. For reasons unknown to Alberto, she excused herself in a low voice, dipping her head, and disappeared into a long hallway bathed in dim light. As Alberto sat himself in the middle of a leather couch, he heard in the distance canned laughter from a television set. The room, full of heavy furniture, was lit only by a single lamp with a large shade, in one corner.

Soon the laughter from the television stopped. In the hallway a light went out, and heavy steps made the floorboards creak. A curly haired colossus appeared in the living room's doorway. He seemed to have emerged from a deep sleep. His face was puffy, he had bags under his small eyes. He approached, limping. Alberto stood to receive his embrace. Unlike his wife, Raúl made no comment on his impromptu visit, just sat down in front of him, massaging his bad leg with one hand. For a long time, during a silence broken only by the squealing of the radiator pipes, Raúl looked about him idly and conspiratorially, as if waiting for something to happen that could provide a distraction.

His wife reappeared, carrying a bottle and two glasses on a tray.

"Some cider?" Raúl asked.

Alberto nodded yes, although he was not really interested in drinking.

The woman leaned over to pour the liquid into the glasses. Raúl took one, got up while looking straight at Alberto, and took a large swallow. Alberto tasted the cider in his turn. The cold liquid relaxed him, did him good. Raúl's wife sat off to the side, in the half-light of the adjoining dining room.

One arm stretched over the back of the couch, the glass of cider balanced on his thigh, Raúl talked about the weather, which he described as a farmer's number one enemy. This cursed, erratic weather that can ruin a whole year's harvest in one night. Then he addressed, sarcastically, the subject of the recent arrival of oats in the region, a grain that was making the fortune of some of his neighbours. He had no illusions, things would unfold as usual: the big players would get rich quick, while the others would get taken to the cleaners.

After about fifteen minutes, in the course of which he listened less to what Raúl was saying than he watched him moving in slow motion, he thought: So this was your best friend, papa? But what did you have in common?

When Raúl went silent, just to keep the conversation going Alberto told him about his father's burial, and then he said right out that he thought the authorities were hiding from him the truth about his death.

Raúl emptied his glass, which made a dull sound when he put it down on the low table. His wife, without his having to give her a sign, came to refill it.

"If I understand you right," Raúl went on, "you're playing detective, is that it?"

Raúl stared at the ceiling for a long time as if calculating how far it was over his head, then puffed out his cheeks to stifle a belch.

"We're going to talk straight to each other, you and me. Okay?"

He half opened his mouth, his eyes on Alberto.

"Now, right now, I'm almost in the street."

He savoured a moment of meaningful silence, and explained, as Pablo had done, half furious and half demoralized, that he had gone in with his father so as to supply more wood to the Araucania Madera Company. He had gone deeply into debt in order to acquire all the necessary equipment, and today, with Roberto's death, the banks were after him, threatening to seize everything he owned, because he couldn't make his monthly payments.

"And I suppose that you, obviously, you can't do anything, right?"

Raúl's wife coughed.

"Raúl, please, the boy has just lost his father."

Raúl's eyes, which were oscillating from barely controlled anger to deep depression, did not leave Alberto.

"You see where I'm at?"

"I'm very sorry."

"Thank you. But your being sorry doesn't help me."

Once again, he left his mouth half open.

"And you know what? Right now, I don't give a damn about your father, or his memory, because I have to keep on, I can't treat myself to eternal rest. And believe me, normally I have a heart, I'm loyal, but when your father began to get all cozy with the Indians, when he tried to . . ."

"Raúl, Raúl," said his wife. "Please . . . Where will this get us?"

One look from her, and he turned away.

"You understand, he didn't want to pay me what he owed me. He'd forgotten that without equipment he was nothing, without my contribution, Araucania Madera would have cut him off. I had no choice. At a certain point, I had to dot the i's, and of course he didn't appreciate that."

When he spoke, he only moved his free hand. It was as if the rest of his body was inanimate.

"He left me in the lurch to go in with the Mapus. He did that to me, who'd known him forever . . ."

He went mute, as though to be sure that Alberto understood the extent of his anger and his pain.

"And you know what? Your father made a fatal mistake. He trusted people you can't trust. They did him in, and for real…"

He opened his mouth to laugh, but no sound came out. And so he started to describe a Saturday at the end of summer, a humid Saturday, bearable only in the shade or at nightfall. He described with lessening animosity, bending down from time to time to grab his glass of cider, the unfolding of a fiesta of the "Mapu," as he called them, as if those two syllables expressed everything he had to say about "those people." It was a fiesta to mark the chief's sixtieth birthday.

"It took place at night, and the men, seated around a picnic table, were drinking like fish, as usual. The women were talking among themselves, and the oldest took care of the food. The children were playing football, there in the middle of the backyard at the chief's house. There was music, doubtless one of those *bachatas* that the Mapu like so much. And Roberto was there, holding the hand of Amalia, the chief's daughter, with whom he was living, and whom he found irresistible. You knew about that, right? Well, Roberto was there, talking with the chief, who according to him, as he told me one day, was 'pragmatic, loyal, and brilliant—' The night went on, the music got louder, and couples started to dance. Roberto dragged Amalia onto the dance floor. And there they were, turning around with the other couples. They danced and danced, and as he had drunk, he got dizzy. But it wasn't unpleasant, he felt like he was on a merry-go-round, like the one we got onto when the circus came to Cunco."

Thanks to the alcohol, Raúl's words, it seemed, were reviving him, rousing him. Seeing Alberto almost as a friend, doubtless aware that his story was interesting him, he picked up the pace even more. And Alberto, despite the constant jibes at the Mapuches and his father, had no trouble imagining Roberto losing control as he swung his hips, as the pine branches turned into spears, and the faces of those not dancing became more and more ghostly. His father was experiencing, and those were apparently his own words, the first signs of fatigue, in particular severe pain in his shoulders and forearms, as if he had just exerted a huge effort.

"And you know what he did, our dear Roberto? Just as they lowered the music for the gift-giving, he gave a sign to one of his workers, for him to roll into the yard a brand new tractor for his good friend, the chief. That met with hearty applause, of course. Because when you give them something, you're their friend. But try to make them understand that they also have to share things from time to time, and you're up against a blank wall. The chief went up to him to embrace him, and whispered in his ear: 'Thank you, but what I really need, is inside you.' That's what he said. I'm not making anything up, it's Roberto who told us all that, right?" he said, turning to his wife, who nodded her head.

119

Now darkness had taken over the yard. The men could no longer hold themselves erect, some were seated, casting about stupidly, others were whimpering and muttering. His eyes heavy, assailed by a headache that was growing worse by the minute, Roberto tripped twice, but he attributed that to the cider. Amalia proposed, in a persuasive voice that was unfamiliar to him, that he lie down on a bed. No dear, she should leave him alone, he just wanted to enjoy himself. When he fell again, he began to laugh, he laughed uncontrollably, as if there could be nothing more hilarious. And *putamadre*, he saw that he had sprained his ankle. Very well, he would do what she wanted, but on condition that she help him. One arm around Amalia's shoulders, he passed through the kitchen, where there were some old women sitting around the table on which were piled pots, dirty plates, and mismatched glasses, then into a bedroom where he let himself drop onto the bed.

"And so," Raúl went on, "Roberto said to the chief's daughter, taking her by the hands, that he never thought he would end his days so happy. He told her that he was ready to do anything for her, agree to anything, make any sacrifice. For the hundredth time, he asked her to give him a child, and as usual she shook her head no. Then he felt like he was being swallowed up by a black hole. He closed his eyes, saw first in his imagination, then in a dream, storms, he glided over dense forests of tall pines and passed through torrents of hail like those that had so impressed him during his years in Quebec. And then he came to earth near a baby carriage, where he made out the angelic face of the child he would never have."

In a calm voice, as if to eschew any superfluous dramatic effect, Raúl said that his father did not open his eyes immediately, certain as he was that his lashes were glued down, and this bizarre idea made him want all of a sudden to get up. The problem was that he couldn't. He saw the sky, a grey sky with puffy clouds lanced by a lost swallow. He saw, and recognized at once, the tops of poplars. A drop of blood came to his mouth, again he tried to stand upright, and this time he lifted his head. *Putamadre*, what was he doing on the ground?

Mesmerized, spellbound, as if the scene were being played out before his eyes, Alberto clearly saw his father lying on the ground, not able to get up. Awkwardly he turned himself around, and it was then that he saw Diego, limp, hanging from a clothesline, like a sheep that had just been bled. His blood ran cold. He remembered that the day after the fiesta, his men had to finish transporting a hundred or so logs from the land at the south end of his property. He peered into the distance, but there was not a single man in sight. Not a single cow. Not a single piece of equipment. ("Those brutes had taken everything, obviously…"). He rolled himself as far as the lawn, collapsed face down on a pile of humid earth, swallowed some of it despite himself, spat for a long time. He had never felt so much pain in his chest. After a few attempts, he was able to unbutton his shirt, and when he saw the scar that, like a snake, zigzagged down his side, he let out a bloodcurdling cry, and began to shake like someone possessed. But what on earth ... He sank back, prone, and stared up at the angry sky that, swirling lower and lower, threatened to swoop down on him. Like an idiot, a thread of saliva escaping from between his teeth, he moaned and muttered, not knowing himself what he was saying.

"Then," continued Raúl, "he crawled to the house. They'd taken everything, of course. The radio, the TV, the refrigerator, the stove. They'd cut the telephone line too, the bastards. He went out, hauled himself as best he could onto a chair, and lost consciousness. During that time, at Araucania Madera, they were waiting for the wood. They waited until the end of the afternoon, and then they phoned me. I found that suspicious, and with two of my men, I went to see what was going on. And I found him there, seated, his arms hanging down, his head thrown back. And when I saw him, I swear," Raúl said, "I thought he was dead. And it's crazy, because I thought immediately of those bloody Indians. Right away. I don't know how many times I'd told him not to trust them. I said: be careful, they're going to have your skin just when you least expect it, that's the way they are. And him: You should get rid of your prejudices ..."

At the hospital, the doctor confirmed what they'd feared, they'd taken a kidney. While they were alone in his room, Roberto, lying on the bed, told Raúl that now the chief's words took on their full meaning: *What I really need is inside you.*

"So can you begin see what they're really like?" said Raúl. "These people are so obliging that they tell you in advance that they're going to do you in. Isn't that marvellous?"

Over the next few days, a representative of the insurance company came and went on Roberto's and Raúl's land, to finally, after long discussions that progressively went downhill, refuse them any compensation. When he left, he even went so far as to say, menacingly, that he suspected them of plundering the farm themselves.

"It's then," interrupted Raúl's wife, "that I told my husband: it's time to put our differences aside. Yes, there were some low blows. Yes, Roberto had played his cards badly, trusting the Mapu so much. But that's enough, otherwise he's going to kill himself. Because yes, your father had got to that point. I went to see him and what I found was a ruined man. Completely finished. He couldn't accept that they'd done that to him."

Alberto, whose hair was standing on end, was nevertheless lost in thought, to the point where for several minutes he could no longer follow what was being said. Bit by bit, an idea, vague at first, became clear and tenacious, and made him uneasy: he could not imagine his father contemplating suicide; that was simply not consistent with the person he was.

"What she says is true," Raúl went on. "I think that if she had not lifted his spirits, he would have hanged himself. Yes sir!"

"One day," Raúl's wife added, "when I was helping him put some order into his house, I said to him: You understand now why Raúl and I have no contact with these people. They're too different. And even there, even after everything they had done to him, he looked at me as if I had just said something incredibly stupid."

"If you ask me, they brainwashed him," said Raúl. "Because they did that to me too. But I wasn't afraid to tell him what I thought: okay, fine, but where is Amalia, can you explain that? Where are your men? Where is your equipment hiding? And above all, where is your kidney, my friend? But him, it's as if he'd given up. He didn't care about anything I said."

Raúl swallowed another glass of cider, and watched Alberto, as if to confirm that he agreed with his version of the facts. And he remembered the equipment he thought he'd seen in the shed adjoining Raúl's house.

"After that, he spent all his time sitting on his porch, watching the sun set. The doctor warned him, the kidney left to him would allow him to live, at the most, four months. I told him: Do what he says, go to the capital for a transplant. But he barely listened. I had the feeling that he didn't want to live any longer, that he was already dead."

"It's true," Raúl's wife broke in. "There was a treatment, but your father didn't want to have anything to do with it. It's sad to say, but it's the truth: he let himself die."

"And you can probably guess the rest," Raúl said. "One afternoon, when I went over there to have him sign some papers, I found him on the ground, at the foot of the chair where he was always sitting. I'd arrived too late. Who knows how many days he'd been there, like that, in that position? Who knows?"

Then, as if there were nothing more to add on the subject, with a casualness that left Alberto breathless, Raúl and his wife began to describe other *retornados* who had fled the *coup d'état* and had come back to the country after the dictatorship was over. Scenarios featuring vaguely idealistic characters, clearly naïve, utterly ignorant of Chilean customs. But of all the stories told to him that night, none could approach the degree of desperation implicit in the last days of his father's life. The *retornados*, thought Alberto, who were so much talked about, so much envied, because, everyone thought, they had come back to the fold with money in their pockets after their little vacation in the lands of the North.

9

That night, he didn't sleep. He wandered from room to room, turned on the radio, went out onto the porch. The enervating chorus of crickets was going full blast. He kept seeing his father crawling like a paraplegic in the middle of the night through a clear-cut forest, he kept hearing the spiteful words of Raúl and his wife.

In the course of the morning, after he'd had something to eat, he saw that Llaima was spewing, like a factory chimney, a thick and constant stream of smoke that darkened the sky, and whose ashen odour was reaching him already. Far off, the volcano growled like thunder. What to do? Estimating the distance between the volcano and the farm, he decided that an eruption of lava would never reach his father's land.

In the afternoon, after having found the property rights to the farm in a shoebox, he got into his pickup and headed towards Cunco. As he approached the small town, grey particles, drifting like snowflakes, covered the windshield. At Cunco, despite the saturated air, life went on as if nothing were happening: itinerant sellers filled the streets, students strolled on the square, and the Mapuches were gathered, as usual, in the doorway of the grocery store at an intersection facing the square. At a stand under a willow tree, Alberto bought an *arrolado* sandwich, and a soft drink. He sat on the back of a bench, his feet on the seat, to bite into the sandwich and watch the people come and go. A dwarf with a pugnacious face and a flattened nose, wearing a jockey cap, brandished a newspaper: *Austral, Austral, todo sobre la elección del Nuevo alcalde…* *Austral, Austral, el Llaima a punto de…* Alberto hailed him. When the newsboy stopped in front of him, Alberto dropped some coins into his sausage-fingered hand. On the front page, Alberto found the smiling and gratified face of Huenchumilla, his tiny eyes behind thick glasses, bright and fatigued. It was the smile of a man who could hardly believe that he had won. However, if he could go by the results, the victory was decisive, a cakewalk even. He scanned the articles on the municipal elections, taking in the new mayor's promise to put an end to four hundred years of apartheid and his vow to attack racism, described as a shameful phenomenon in a country like ours!

He left the paper on the bench, went up to a garbage container to throw away the empty can, and stepped onto the sidewalk. When he turned around, he saw an urchin six or seven years old, on the tips of his toes, reaching his arm into the garbage to pull out the can. Behind the tangle of pine branches he located the bank with its imposing oak door, and he entered the establishment.

After a long wait, a man in a striped three-piece suit came to a halt in front of him, a grimace engraved on the lower part of his face. He followed a maze of beige corridors, adorned with paintings of idyllic southern landscapes. A mahogany desk loomed at the end of a vast office. A window gave onto a garden with a fountain, where a few sparrows splashed about. Seated, Alberto became aware of the soft strains of baroque music. The banker, impeccably dressed, with delicate features and fine manners, rested his elbows on the desk, and embarked on a tribute to his father. He was, the man assured him, a hard-working, honest, dedicated man, full of compassion. A kind of old-fashioned idealist, was he not? He didn't wait for a reply, but added, his eyes half closed, "All my sympathies."

Alberto informed him of his intention to sell the farm before returning to Canada, given that he was, along with his brother (who, settled in São Paulo, would be sending him a proxy), the legal heir.

The banker blinked, the corners of his mouth quivering, as though he expected this to be some sort of joke. Seeing that Alberto made no move, he cleared his throat, his fist in front of his mouth, more to hide his amusement than as a mark of politeness.

"But Mr. Ventura," he ventured in a suave voice, "where have you been for the last twenty-four hours? Have you not seen what's going on out there? Are you not aware that Llaima is threatening to swallow everything up?"

At first Alberto didn't know how to respond. After a long pause he came to his own defence, saying that yes, of course, he had seen that the volcano was about to erupt. But the banker cut him off: he would be making a serious strategic error if he were to divest himself of the farm at this time. And he launched into a detailed description of the disastrous consequences for real estate in the region of Puerto Montt after the eruption of the Chaitén volcano about a year earlier.

"The sector where your father's farm is located was highly prized five or six years ago," he said. "People fought then to acquire fertile land near the Huichahue River, with its deep bed and pure water. Some profited by it, and made fortunes with oats. But your father and some others gambled everything on their relationship with the forestry companies, and that did not give the results they hoped for."

Wrinkles appeared on his forehead.

"We here at the Bank of the South were the first financial institution, through the division we set up to offer aid to our agricultural partners, to warn against an irresponsible cultivation of eucalyptus. This tree, with its phenomenal growth and undeniable qualities, has in recent years, as you have no doubt seen with your own eyes, done irreparable damage in some parts of the region. You have to understand that once it has been planted, it takes ten to fifteen years for the ground to recover. It's a serious problem, and some did not take the problem seriously."

Alberto could not believe his ears. At the beginning of the 1990s, when his father took over the farm, this same bank had lent him money at preferential rates because he was going to plant eucalyptus.

"Why do you think empires like Araucania Madera pay others to supply them with wood?"

The banker stretched his arms as if to draw down his sleeves.

"Take my word for it, they're not worth very much," he stated, in a voice that broached no appeal.

And he raised his arched eyebrows as far as they would go. Alberto remained speechless.

"And what do you advise me to do?"

As if the banker were happy to see Alberto listening to reason, he bestowed upon him a smile of apparent concern.

"First, cross your fingers that Llaima doesn't spill its lava onto your land. And second, keep your rights to the property and come back for a tour of the region ... in ten years. If I'm still here, it would give me great pleasure to discuss matters with you at that time. Believe me, that's the best thing to do. It will enable you to save time, energy, and money.

BACK AT THE FARM, even though he was exhausted, he spent most of the afternoon monitoring Llaima, whose crater was still belching out just as much smoke, but no lava as yet. In his head he tried again to measure the distance between the volcano and the farm, alarmed by a speleologist he'd heard earlier on the radio, who stated that lava from an eruption could spread over a radius of more than thirty kilometres.

THAT NIGHT, WITH THE SHOTGUN on the rear seat of the pickup, he drove slowly. The engine made the dashboard shudder, and the heater slowly dissipated the condensation that had formed a mock continent on the windshield. In the middle of an endless night, he crossed some railway tracks, then he drove for a long time in a straight line without meeting a single vehicle. He saw in the distance the confusing jumble of small houses, and the shaggy tops of the *rucas*. He took a nameless road that kept altering course, and seemed to be the village's main street. Behind the lit window of a house, silhouettes moved back and forth in the intermittent bluish light from a television set. A woman in a long dress was walking falteringly, like a sleepwalker, on the sidewalk on the other side of the street. In front of a building where a naked light bulb was hanging from a cord, men in undershirts were talking, and softly laughing.

HE PARKED THE TRUCK in front of a small empty park, where in the darkness he thought he could make out some swings. On foot, he passed some modest bungalows in front of which toys, or sometimes piles of metal, lay scattered. He came to a square dimly lit by two streetlights. A few steps away from an impressive *rewe* representing Mapuche gods, an old man was lost in thought, sitting alone on a stone bench.

Alberto watched him. He went up to the man, who did not bother to look at him, and sat down on the same bench. Yes, his stature, diminutive as that of a child, matched the portraits sketched out by Noemi and Raúl. His hair was smooth and silvered, his eyes fixed and shining like that of a blind man, while his mouth with its delicate lips exhaled a light mist when he breathed. But of course, he thought all at once, it's the man he saw at his father's funeral!

He then realized that he'd forgotten the shotgun in the pickup.

"I knew you'd come sooner or later," said the chief, still without turning towards him.

At their feet, miniature cyclones of dust swirled feebly.

"It's a good thing, this little wind," he went on. "It's pushing the smoke towards the mountains. So you've moved into your father's house?"

Alberto cleared his throat. He had come to shed light on his death.

"You know, I had great esteem for you father. That is why my daughter and I came to pay our respects and express our gratitude the other day. My deepest sympathies, my boy."

Alberto looked at him, incredulous.

133

"Of course, people must have said all sorts of things about us. It doesn't surprise me, and it's of no importance, because you are here now."

He smiled kindly, and held out his hand while slightly bowing his head. His name was Don Francisco. As he spoke to him in a voice astonishingly like that of a child, Alberto observed his bright eyes, his delicate features, his tanned complexion, the colour of earth, attesting to whole days exposed to the sun, and he told himself that there was no mistaking that face. He had something of the Mapuches' shyness, their uneasiness and wariness in the company of a *huinca*. Still, he tried talking to him naturally, without looking at him, but with that dose of familiarity typical of people in the South. He spoke to him about daily life, about the unpredictable weather, a constant enemy, about women who complained too much (at that point a smile appeared, darting to the left side of his face), about corn harvests, as disappointing as those of the previous year...

After a time, Alberto was only half listening. When the chief paused at last, as if to catch his breath, Alberto cut him off:

"Excuse me, I need to know... How did my father die? Can you tell me?"

Alberto was there, listening, hoping that this was the right time and place, hoping that this man would throw open the door to the truth, and that he'd be able, once and for all, to rid himself of the anguish he'd been carrying around with him for days, like an angry monkey perched on his shoulder. He was so engrossed that he was unaware of the pleading in his voice, to which Don Francisco also seemed impervious, since, without being asked, in a pleasing, almost amicable tone, he journeyed back in time, paused at a day of dreary rain, stammered, shut his eyes for a moment, and then continued on further back to a fiesta at his house, the one spoken of by Noemi, when Roberto met Amalia.

And then, Alberto noticed, the chief began to gesture with his hands in an attempt to find the right word, and sometimes, surprisingly, he faltered ... Was he lying? After a while Alberto became convinced that he was omitting entire scenes, but he was also certain that it was not intentional. And so, trying to read between the lines, he saw in his mind's eye a Don Francisco who, astonished, watched a smiling and affable Roberto enter his yard for the first time. He saw the chief, who studied him without moving, the expression on his face shifting from disbelief to amazement, from incredulity to a nascent anger, while about him people came and went holding plastic glasses, and children dodged around the adults, running after a scruffy soccer ball. He saw Roberto asking who was the chief. A neighbour at the other end of the yard, in the middle of the celebrants, pointed at Don Francisco, in the half-light that was closing in like a curtain. He saw Roberto looking at the chief, hesitating, then approaching with a brimming glass of cider in his hand. Roberto held out his hand, and for a few moments Don Francisco let it hang there to no avail, taking pleasure, it seemed, in his rudeness, staring Roberto down. When the chief finally grasped his hand, he drew him gently in, and murmured:

"I don't like this kind of game, I don't like it at all..."

Roberto drew himself up.

"But I don't understand, it's you who... At least, that's what the boy said who came to see me at the farm," he objected, pointing to a scrawny child with a round face behind the chief, whose silhouette came and went among the other youngsters.

"I'm sorry? What are you saying?"

And Don Francisco, Alberto said to himself, began thinking very fast, and looked around him, trying to understand what could have happened, and how at the same time he could bring an end to this annoying conversation. It was then that, purely by chance, his eyes lit on Amalia, standing in the kitchen doorway. She stood erect wearing a brown skirt that covered her knees, following her father with that look of apprehension and expectation that he knew so well, that look that she had first adopted in adolescence when she began to live a double life—a double life she never revealed to her mother when she was still of this world.

"I thought perhaps we were going to talk business."

"Ah, yes? Excuse me," said Don Francisco, raising a hand as if to stop the wind.

And with long strides he walked straight to his daughter, discreetly motioning to her to join him in the kitchen. This scene, in the blue half-light smelling of fried food, amid a clutter of dirty glasses, silverware, and piles of chipped and dirty plates, the chief recalled, but with a smile, as if to excuse his fit of anger. Several times he repeated, in his defence:

"She'd never said a thing to me. You understand? Not a word. She'd sent little Juanito to your father's farm, without breathing a word to me."

So there was a confrontation between father and daughter. What did she want, for God's sake? the chief insisted. Had she already forgotten what that man had done? The pain he'd caused to the family of Matias, the boy who worked for him and whom he'd killed? What had got into her? Alberto imagined him advancing on his daughter, beside himself: why had she done that, especially during the Nguillatún celebrations? Was she trying to provoke him, to hurt him, *trewa kodo*!

When celebrants came in to the kitchen, Don Francisco ignored them, and continued to upbraid her and to demand explanations.

At first her only response was to shrug her shoulders, and with this gesture, thought Alberto, she was telling the truth. She didn't really know why she had invited that man. Then, clearly not knowing what she was going to say, she began to describe that humid day, with its blinding light, a light that, in summer, made the poplars' branches shimmer in slow motion. She was walking, dazed by the heat, and fascinated, as usual, by the contrast between the cool grey of the slumping bushes' shadows and the incandescence of the indigo sky. At first, when she saw the black vehicle that, like a hallucination, appeared down the road, aqueous and improbable, she didn't think much of it. Even though she wasn't really looking, absorbed as she was in her thoughts, going over in her head the assignments on which she had been working the day before. What caused problems with the mucous membrane? Was glycerol essential when inserting a sperm straw for insemination? She raised her eyes, and doubtless that's when she saw, thought Alberto, the sun glinting off the chrome on the black American van. That furtive but ostentatious reflection that would remain fixed in her memory, much more than Roberto's serene and quietly complacent manner, his elbow resting on the window frame as he took her in without any sense of embarrassment. Yes, without her being aware of it, it was the elusive, multi-hued mirage-like reflection that had captivated her. In fact, it was only days later, perhaps even a week, that this spellbinding reflection came back to her, accidentally, thanks to another reflection, at the university, when a door opened in front of her. Afterwards, Alberto told himself, when she thought about it as she was coming out of a class in bovine biology, she realized that she had no idea why she was so obsessed in this way. Running after a *micro*, she took her courage in both hands and faced her demons: how old was she, for God's sake? Was she an imbecile, or what? To be so fascinated by a vulgar black car with a man at the wheel who devoured her with his eyes? Was he really devouring her with his eyes? She wasn't even sure. She spent whole days talking to herself out loud, cursing herself under her breath.

She invented a thousand excuses to go near Roberto's farm. She had to visit a childhood friend who lived close by, to gather *canelo* twigs in the nearby forest, to buy ears of corn from one of Roberto's neighbours. And always she kept an eye on the goings on at the farm, noting that they worked hard there, and that there was no woman in sight. One day, near the gate, she approached two young men who worked there, and inquired, without seeming to, about their working conditions and the boss's behaviour. She learned that he was demanding but loyal, that he often needed a veterinarian but he didn't often call for one, the visits being too costly. At the end of the conversation, the men asked her if she was looking for work. Smiling, she said no, that she still had two and a half years left at the university. Afterwards, she often, during the afternoons, imagined herself arriving at Roberto's farm in a van to discuss with him the hypothetical respiratory problems of calves. And she saw herself explaining how to keep the stable air fresh: eliminating dust, water vapour, and harmful gases such as ammonia, methane, and carbon dioxide.

"But if you really want to know," continued Don Francisco, "it seemed to me that what she wanted from your father was to get away. In fact, I always felt that she was ill at ease with us, that she had her eyes set too much on the *huincas*, if you know what I mean."

That night, in the chief's backyard, cowed by his anger, Amalia swore up and down that she would keep her distance from Roberto.

Every time Roberto tried to approach the chief, he turned his back on him, called one of his children, took a lively interest in what the women were saying. Then, at a certain point, curious to know who Roberto was talking to, the chief sought him out, but he had already disappeared. And so what Noemi had told him, that Don Francisco had introduced his daughter to Roberto, was that all nonsense?

"You know," said the chief, "we're like that, the Mapuches. We forget nothing. Maybe that's why our elders said that the past was a burden to them."

"You're talking about what?" asked Alberto. "My father's young worker?"

"Young Matias's death was terrible. It shook us. Me, in particular. His mother was my neighbour. But that's not all, you know. A long time ago, you may never have heard about it, one of our people was trampled by your grandfather's horse."

"I knew about it."

They looked at each other. A glimmer of defiance shone deep in the chief's eyes.

Against the wishes of her father, Amalia continued to hover around Roberto's farm. One day the chief learned, through one of his neighbours, that his daughter was now working for that man. Weeks later, an acquaintance of his daughter told him that Amalia and the man were seeing each other, and that in the evenings they paraded through the streets of Temuco, hand in hand. He was filled with anger, but what could he do? Confront his daughter? He'd never known how to talk to her. So they came to a tacit agreement: when they passed each other at night within the house walls, rank and oozing humidity, they avoided mentioning that man. Only once she opened her heart (and it was then that he understood how deep were his daughter's feelings for this White man) and begged him to forgive the man for what he had done. Had he not taught her to have the wisdom to forgive? He didn't answer, and she took the message: never again would she try to rehabilitate him in his eyes.

Over the following two years, Roberto did everything in his power to help the Mapuche village. He convinced the bureaucrats of the Cunco commune to repair the chronic water leaks in the crumbling aqueduct system. What is more, and this was his real triumph, he persuaded those same bureaucrats to free up funds for the construction of a small clinic.

How had his father achieved all that, Alberto asked himself, with no connections in the region? He thought again of his Aunt Noemi. Why had she not said anything? To protect his reputation? Because she was appalled by the influence trafficking and the little ploys that undermined the system?

One Saturday afternoon, as a blazing sun turned the inside of the chief's living room into an oven, there was a knock at the door. Amalia went to open it, and sitting at the table, leafing through *Austral*, the chief looked up to find Roberto on the doorstep, standing in an inferno of dust and stagnant air. He watched him as, head lowered, hands in his pants pockets, he entered the house. Amalia and the man stood side by side, awkward and timid as adolescents.

It was she who spoke, first reminding her father of all that Roberto had done for the community. She could no longer continue this way, without his consent, without being able to share with him what she was living with her lover. She had decided to go and live with Roberto, but she didn't want to slam the door, she wanted him to support her, and once and for all to forgive her man his past errors.

The light from the window blinded the chief, so much so that he had to turn his eyes away. In a muffled voice, he told his daughter that she could take her belongings, that he never wanted to see her again. Roberto then intervened, but seeing the expression on Don Francisco's face, he cut himself short in the middle of a sentence. Large tears fell onto Amalia's navy blue T-shirt, as she packed her suitcase and softly closed the door behind her.

Don Francisco would never have believed that no longer seeing his daughter would cause him such suffering. He would never have believed that passing her without saying a word would be so painful. He admitted all this to Alberto.

Exactly nine months later it was he who, on a Sunday afternoon in autumn under a cloudless sky, paid a visit to Roberto's farm. He climbed the sinuous path leading to the house, and as he approached, the dogs roused themselves from their torpor and began barking sleepily. She came to the door. Suddenly she was beautiful to him, mature, full of confidence. For a long moment, standing next to the rubber doormat, none of the three said a word. Looking about him, Don Francisco told them that after a visit to the Pehuenches, a Mapuche community in the mountains, he contracted a serious infection and had to have a kidney removed. As a result, he had for months been suffering from kidney failure.

"But you have to get treatment, Papa!" cried Amalia, dismayed, immediately forgetting their quarrel.

"I've been promised a kidney, but I've been waiting for months. It seems there's nothing to be done. Meanwhile, I can't function with all my vomiting, I'm always dizzy, and my morale... To be honest, I don't think I'll see the summer..."

Amalia's eyes opened wide.

Again, the three of them stood there, silent.

"But I'll give you one of my kidneys, and that will be it!"

Casting his eyes around him again, the chief, in a weak voice, thanked his daughter politely, but as if to discourage her in her desire to help him, he reminded her that for a transplant to succeed, the blood types had to be compatible.

And then he continued to stare at the stable, the corrals, the tractors parked every which way in front of the kitchen coop, the poplars lining the road, as if to imply that he had come only to deliver the news.

After a few formalities, he turned around and left, his progress now unsteady.

The next morning, Amalia made her way to the hospital in Cunco. When a nurse told her that she did not have the same blood type as her father, she was devastated, said Don Francisco. Everyone could see that she was performing her tasks on the farm like a sleepwalker, lost in thought, sometimes short-tempered. One night, as Roberto himself told the chief, while the couple was at the dinner table and the teapot was steaming on the wood stove, he asked Amalia what they might possibly do for her father. Her only response, without even looking at him, was to go and shut herself up in the bedroom.

Two weeks went by, with Amalia consumed by an anxiety that was slowly poisoning her relationship with Roberto.

One day, Don Francisco continued, while Roberto was in Cunco on business, he went to a private clinic behind the church on the square, in a low building, all steel and glass. When the doctor asked him for his blood type, he found it ironic that he, the former head of a hospital, did not have that information. A nurse took a blood sample, and he learned that he was O-, in other words a universal donor. Through the doctor, Roberto established contact with a kidney specialist in Temuco, who the same day reassured him: if he was in good health it was possible, yes, to live with one kidney.

One Saturday morning he told this to Amalia, Don Francisco said. First she was surprised, and then, as if having second thoughts, she became glum again and asked him, curtly, why he had taken those steps.

"Why do you think?"

Slowly she rose, went around the small kitchen table, making the floor creak, stroked the back of his neck, and planted a long tender kiss on his lips.

One cold night, the couple knocked at Don Francisco's door. For almost two hours, sitting around the table in the main room, Roberto tried to persuade the chief to accept his offer, while Amalia gazed adoringly at her lover with bright eyes full of admiration, turning from time to time towards her father, as if to say: You see how you were mistaken. You understand now what he's really like ...

Don Francisco protested several times that the day he'd gone to visit them, he'd had no intention of making such a request. But Roberto did not relent: he'd never been so sure of anything in his life.

"I understood on that day that he was doing it out of love for my daughter," said the chief. He wanted to tell her: See, you can never any more doubt my sincerity. But for me, it was clear, he was also doing it so as no longer to have young Matias's death on his conscience. You know, the Mapuche labourer who worked for him."

Alberto half-opened his mouth: the chief was right, his father wanted to redeem himself. In God's name, did you succeed, papa? Did the memory of that boy stop haunting you? As Alberto listened to Don Francisco's story, in his mind, superimposed on the apocalyptic scene painted by Raúl of his father's loss of a kidney, were the ambulance headlights that, in the dark of night, appeared like two eyes. The white van stopped in front of the village clinic his father had helped build. Two men got down from the vehicle. One wore a white smock, the other a short-sleeved shirt. They rolled their machines up to the clinic.

"You understand," said the chief, "I didn't want to get the institutions involved in that. They always complicate everything, they understand nothing about our way of doing things. They're so quick to accuse us of all sorts of wrongdoing. And then, your father knew a kidney specialist in Temuco who put him in contact with a surgeon who, for a price, agreed to come."

Seconded by the ambulance driver who assisted him as a nurse, the surgeon, a young man of few words, bent over Roberto, while behind, pacing up and down, a *machi* intoned a lament to the accompaniment of a *kultrún*.

"What happened to the equipment? At the end of his life, Roberto saw the error he'd made in dealing with that company, you know, Araucania something-or-other. But to sever the connection had its consequences. He had to break with an old acquaintance, someone rather unsavoury, who didn't want him to terminate his partnership with the company. There were attempts at intimidation, of sabotage, and of course we supported Alberto."

Suddenly Alberto saw, at the entry to the farm, Raúl spitting words in his father's face. And he remembered Raúl's shed, with its cranes and its chainsaws.

"I said to your father: Let him have his machines, your friend. We'll make out. Strange as it may seem, many people began to resent him just because he spent time with us. What do you want, that's the way people are around here."

And a few minutes later, knowing that Alberto only wanted to know one thing, Don Francisco said:

"What I want to tell you is that your father was doing well, after having had the unbelievable generosity to make me the gift that he did. And then one day Amalia left for Cunco on a shopping trip and she came back to find him on the ground in front of the house, in very bad shape. We did everything to save him ... What had happened? In any case, I know that your father's stitches were reopened, to make it look like it was a medical complication that had caused his death."

During this long conversation, Alberto several times recognized his father in the various scenes described by Don Francisco ("Roberto was a fighter, a force of nature.

But for me he was above all a man alone, who felt he had always been abandoned...") There was no doubt: he had known him well and appreciated him. For her part, since Roberto's death, Amalia had left for Temuco, where she was living with someone she knew, while looking for a room to rent. Apparently she was determined to continue her education. When Alberto expressed his wish to meet her, Don Francisco was quick to discourage him.

"She's not ready, you'll have to give her time. Fortunately she's young, and she'll be able to rebuild her life, not so?"

The chief went silent, and Alberto felt that he had nothing more to say. After a moment, they rose, and before separating, they shook hands without saying goodbye.

ALBERTO DROVE BACK, his eyes on the road, but not really seeing it. He felt that he had at last come to know his father, through all the characters he had played in the course of his life. According to Don Francisco, his father had found some serenity in his last years, and was no longer a puppeteer manipulating those around him. Perhaps that was it, the logical outcome of his life: to rid himself of the Machiavellian view of the world that had poisoned his existence.

But right away, he began to have his doubts: was he accepting the chief's account of his father because it would rehabilitate him in his own eyes? And why ignore all the gaps, the approximations, all the implausibilities even, in the chief's story? *Putamadre*, what was true in all that? Who found his father's body? Amalia? Raúl? He began to smell smoke and thought at first that the engine was giving out. Seeing nothing unusual on the dashboard, he told himself that it was perhaps farmers nearby burning garbage or hay. When the headlights could no longer penetrate the clouds of smoke, he realized that it couldn't only be dust. He lowered the driver's window, and after inhaling a lungful of the smoke's pungent odour, he rolled it up again.

He slowed down. Surrounded by a thick spiralling cloud, he was barely able to see the poplars bordering the road. A bit farther on, despite the fact that the windows were closed, he heard branches cracking, and for the first time he thought about a forest fire. He climbed the valley leading to the farm, passed slowly in front of Raúl's house, intact, and made out, scattered over the property, a dozen cranes and chainsaws. ("Yes, he took them all and blamed it on the Mapuches…") He went down the little incline, and finally, now filled with panic, saw the tops of the flames which, like hungry fingers, were eating away at the eastern part of the farm. He drove alongside the fields to the north, heedless of whether the fire might reach him. When he stopped the vehicle at the farm's entrance, in front of the hallucinatory and unreal spectacle of the land ablaze, he thought about Llaima. But the volcano was sleeping far off, stately and peaceful.

Alberto got out, and despite the fierce heat, barely endurable, despite the thick smoke that stung his eyes, he sat on the truck's hood to climb onto the roof. He realized, stunned, that only his father's land was on fire. An accident? A criminal act? *Putamadre*, who had done that? He thought of Raúl, Araya, Pedro, and also a young Mapuche crawling under barbed wire, nimble and imagined, sent by the chief while they were talking together. A Mapuche way of purifying land with fire? When the roof of the house caved in, and he saw in the distance what was left of it enveloped in flames, his eyes grew moist. But he stayed put until the wooden and barbed wire fence could no longer contain the fire's assault. He stayed because he felt that he was witnessing the end of something, the death of part of himself. He remembered the story his grandfather liked to tell him when he was a child: the story of a family born in Andalusia more than seven hundred years earlier, and that had to flee one day to Macedonia, only to cross the Atlantic some centuries later because of wars and stupid persecutions, to settle, without really knowing where it had come to, in a pastoral land whose splendours held the promise of a radiant future.